ON THE EDGE
Selected short Stories

Patrick Belshaw

BLACKTHORN PRESS

Blackthorn Press, Blackthorn House
Middleton Rd, Pickering YO18 8AL
United Kingdom

ISBN 978 1 906259 51 8

© Patrick Belshaw

In
memory of
my wife, Kathie,
who was my first reader
for a number of these stories

INTRODUCTION

'Always in the short story,' wrote Frank O'Connor in *The Lonely Voice*, 'there is this sense of outlawed figures wandering about the fringes of society.'

It is not difficult to see where this view comes from: a substantial number of short stories do in fact feature characters from what he goes on to call a 'submerged population'. However, the case is over-stated in that it appears to take no account of the obvious observation that life's journey can drive all of us to the fringes, perhaps even to the edge, from time to time. Most are driven there by illness, bereavement, dislocation, or some other adversity; but there are a few who are confined, if not to the edge, at least to a path a little away from it, by virtue of some special gift or condition with which they have been blessed (or cursed?) almost from the moment of birth. There are others of course, another minority, who are close to the edge by choice, who seem to revel in life at the sharp end – almost as if, when operating close to death or disaster, they are able to feel most alive.

It is hardly by chance that short story writers in particular find themselves circling around this *fringe* territory, drawn again and again to focus on characters who are attempting to cope with intense life experiences. My work is no exception. I am mindful of all those people out there who, for whatever reason, find themselves on the edge, on the fringe, at the margins. Like my characters, they will cope in varying degrees. Some may fail: fail others, fail themselves. Some may fall. And some may even perish. But because we know that we all have to fall at some point, perhaps what really matters is the nature of the 'clinging on': the dignity displayed in the struggle. Aspects of the way this struggle plays out lend themselves to what V.S. Pritchett has described as 'the glancing form' of the short story, a form which differs from that of the novel principally by being rooted, as Walter Allen has suggested, 'in a single incident or perception' – which might remind us of Elizabeth Bowen's simple definition of the genre: 'a narrative with a beginning, a crisis, and an end'.

* * *

In one form or another, I have been writing all my life. There have been modest successes along the way, but publication is not really why I write. I write because most of the time I enjoy writing. I write because the thought of not writing disturbs me. (When my dear wife died in 2009, I was blocked for almost three years – and it was like a double bereavement.) Crucially, I write because it seems to fulfil a need in me. Whether this need is concerned with anxiety in some way, I do not know – and anyway there are conflicting views about how this might work. Of poetry (which is similar in process to short story writing) Harold Bloom has expressed the view that 'a poem is not an overcoming of anxiety, but *is* that anxiety', whereas T.S. Eliot took a different stance: 'an artist's writing is not the expression of personality, but an escape from personality'.

What I do know, at this advanced stage of my life, is that I find myself writing because I want my work to be part of the legacy I leave to my wonderful family and friends. Not, I hasten to add, because I am greatly proud of what I have written (I think I know my place in the canon) but because my writing is very much a part of who I am, and therefore it will be a part of what they will remember me by – along with all the other bits of quirkiness!

* * *

I have written around eighty short stories, so to select just twenty for this volume has left me with some difficult choices. Of the twenty stories finally chosen, ten have been published previously – seven in

v

entirety, two in extract form and one as an earlier version. My title for this selection, *On the Edge,* is not only thematic, it might also serve to remind us that it is our edges that define us. 'Without edges,' wrote Louise LeBrun, 'we would not be recognizable as different or distinct from our environments. Without edges, we would blend into our surroundings . . . disappear . . . become part of something else and no longer be who we are.'

By now I should know who I am. I am an individual traveller along the way – yes, sometimes struggling with the vicissitudes of life, but mostly delighting in the wonder of it all. I also happen to be something of a writer.

Patrick Belshaw

CONTENTS

On the Edge   1
The Disfigurement   11
The Photograph   17
The Discoverers   23
The Tribute   25
Griselle   35
Grey's Elegy   46
The Crossing   54
A Darker Shade of Night   62
The Bird House   68
The Falling Man   85
Following Balloons   96
The Vicar   106
Come Into my Parlour   113
Fly Fishing   120
Finding a Piece of Sky   128
A Change in the Landscape   140
By Aventure   147
Las Orejas   161
No Need of Words   173

ON THE EDGE

"What on earth am I doing here?" Liz thought. "Whatever possessed me to agree to this? Why didn't I just tell him to piss off, get the hell out of my life? Yes – give your precious Monica a call. Stick *her* on a bloody rock face!"

She was so angry. Only the thought of the twins was keeping her going. Your first year at university could be tough enough without worrying about your father and his mid-life crisis. "Mid-life crisis, my arse! What a pathetic excuse for getting your leg over some airhead half your age."

Pete had climbed quickly, transferring his weight with the ease of a dancer. He was soon calling down to say that he was taking in the slack.

"That's me," she cried, when the rope tugged at her harness.

As she waited for the instruction to climb, she twanged the rope with a finger. It was comfortingly taut. This was her lifeline: her umbilical cord. The thought amused her at first. And then she got to thinking that from now on, right to the end of the climb, she would be attached to him. She wouldn't – no, couldn't – make a move without him. He was in complete control. She was in his power, at his mercy. Was that why he had suggested this outing? To allow him to regain some of the control he reckoned he had lost recently? No, that was silly. Fanciful thinking. This was just a climb. This was the nature of the sport: two people joined together for their safety. Mutually dependent, if anything.

Yet the thought occurred to her again, fleetingly, once she was on the move. There he was, above her, in total control, talking her up, suggesting the moves – like a chess master – encouraging, coaxing, congratulating; and all the time, taking in the long umbilical cord between them. Shortening it at this point. But sometimes lengthening it. Sometimes tying it off in places. Hopefully, never severing it.

A few seconds after having these thoughts, she lost her footing. Instantly, firmly – as if to underline the control she had been musing on – he held her. She dropped a mere inch or two. No more than the stretch of the rope permitted.

"I've got you," he called down.

"Good," she cried. She was reassured.

When she reached his stance and was expertly tied on, she quickly recovered both her breath and her composure. She felt completely safe, tucked into the 'sentry box', as he called it, her cord attached to the placental bough of an ancient holly tree – so secure, so relaxed, in fact, that surprisingly she felt able to look out.

The view was magnificent. Not just the valley below, and the hills beyond, layered in darkening shades of blue, but the sky above. She fancied herself almost level with two clouds that were drifting slowly across the sky. No, it was one cloud really, for she could see now that they were linked by a narrow isthmus of vapour. She watched fascinated. Would the isthmus get wider or narrower? Would one section be cast adrift? She found herself caring. Why was that, she wondered?

"What are those two peaks?" she asked, breaking the spell. She was pointing to two domed-shaped summits just visible in the distance.

"Ah, they're the Paps," he grinned.

"Really?" she said. "The Paps – honestly?" He nodded. "Trust you climbers!"

"Well, you must admit they're aptly-named," he said, turning his smile on her again. "Except there are actually three of them. You can't see the lowest one from here." He paused a moment, before taking himself out of the belay system. "Yes," he continued, his eyes

2

twinkling in that roguish fashion of his, "that's one well-endowed lady."

She could see at that moment how attractive other women might find him. And if anything, he was more attractive now than he was when they had first met all those years ago as students. Slate-blue eyes set in a craggy, weathered face; athletic body (no sign of a pot, damn him); full of vigour; bounding with energy; relaxed, confident, easy-going, good-humoured: she could go on. An air of danger about him, too. A lot of women fell for that. She among them.

She took in the full view again. You really noticed things up here, she marvelled. You had time; you had space. You had little else to distract you. And, level with large birds playing the thermals – what were they: hawks? Buzzards? – you had a strong sense of freedom. She could see what the attraction had been for him all these years. Getting somewhere – somewhere dangerously difficult – by the sweat of your brow, your skill, your technical competence, your daring; and having got there – no, even *on the way* there – this feeling of peace and serenity, this feeling of being a part of the rock you climbed, the air you breathed – the same air that held up the gliding birds – the cloud you moved through, the sun that laid a warm hand on your body. Suddenly, she felt jealous – not of that Monica, but of him, and the job he did, and the life he led: the life that had meant so much to him.

Even though Pete kept her on a tight rope, she found the next two pitches very difficult – mainly because she was climbing up an airy buttress. She now understood the meaning of something that climbers seemed to thrive on: exposure. There was no looking out at the view during these sections. The same was true at the tight belay station between the two pitches. She preferred to stay close to the rock, looking in, examining its colour and texture, quite happy to concede that she was no climber.

The following pitch was technically no easier; but she felt more comfortable with it because she felt less exposed. When she eventually completed the final move, she was surprised to find herself on a little terrace covered in vegetation.

"Fancy a snack?" he grinned, as he led her to the spike belay in the wall of rock behind him. And, like a magician producing something from a hat, he presented her with a handful of bilberries.

"Thanks," she cried, licking her dry lips. "A real life-saver."

They guzzled dozens of the fat, ripe berries from the heap he had assembled on the rock shelf below his belay. Sucking them up from the palms of their hands, they looked at one another and laughed together – for the first time in weeks – as the purple juice ran down their chins, leaving them, lips stained, looking like a couple of serious heart cases.

He really was trying very hard to please; she had to give him that. Hopefully it wasn't all a big act. No, she was sure it wasn't. To be fair, this was Pete all over. He had always been kind, naturally thoughtful. Despite all the hurt, despite all her anger, this she had to concede. And he was generous, too. To a fault. Perhaps that had been his downfall?

He took the opportunity of space on the terrace to run the rope through his hands. She was fascinated by the way he handled it: firmly, but almost caressingly – like the way he had once handled her body. Hers, she thought – and also Monica's? Oh, would it ever go away, this cloud that hung over them?

It was at the next belay point that she noticed a shift in the weather. Although the sun was still shining down in the valley, spotlighting the farm and their little campsite, the sky above them, over the unseen summit, was changing from dark to black even as she watched. The blackness spread quickly, like an inkblot, eventually seeping across the whole of the sky and shutting out the sun. She shivered. Peter was out of sight and out of earshot. She was suddenly feeling cold and lonely.

4

There was a rumble of thunder. She shivered again as she scanned the rock face above her. Another roll of thunder grumbled in the belly of the sky; it sounded closer this time. The rope had become inactive – Pete had obviously reached the belay – so she removed her hands and chafed some warmth into her arms. A sound from above – a strange, slithering sound, as if something was sliding down the rock – suddenly gained her attention. She grabbed the rope and looked up anxiously. "Oh, no! He hasn't fallen? Please, please, don't let him fall," she said out loud. In a second her fear changed to a stabbing sickness as she saw a fast-moving shape, arms thrown out, coming down towards her. She braced herself for the impact – only to find herself clutching at Peter's waterproof jacket which, tied to a line, he had lowered down to her. There he was again, anticipating her every need – or perhaps (her relief had made her fanciful) responding sensitively to the shivers vibrating along that umbilical cord. The thunder rolled again. She donned the jacket eagerly, adjusting it just in time to respond to the sharp tug on her harness.

"That's me," she cried, gratefully.

The first spots of rain began to fall as she set off to climb the next pitch. She could feel the rope not only tight but pulling at her as she made her first few moves. Peter was obviously assisting her, and she wasn't offended. The thunder was getting louder and there were now distant flashes of lightning. An exposed rock face was no place to hang about on with an electric storm almost upon them.

She reached his stance – a mere cleft in the rock – to be greeted by a dramatic flash of lightning that unzipped the sky above them, followed a few seconds later by a frightening roll of thunder. As he tied her on, there was yet another dazzling flash, followed almost immediately this time by a deafening clap. The storm was almost overhead. He pulled on the rope, shortening her belay, moving her further into the cleft. He was smiling with his mouth, trying to appear unconcerned; but there was anxiety in his eyes, she thought.

5

"Oughtn't we to turn back?" she asked.

"I think not," he laughed. "Only two more pitches to go. Short ones, too. Forty-five minutes, max. Going back down would take well over two hours. Supposing we could do it, that is. Tricky business – reversing a climb."

It was now raining hard: cold, needling rain from somewhere so high up that it probably began as hail. He pushed her right up into the cleft, moving in over her in a wide-legged straddle position, shielding her from the rain, as he detached himself from the belay system and prepared to climb. She wondered, as she took the rope from him, what he had been standing on all this time. Then, as he moved upwards to begin the climb, she saw the narrowest of footholds, one on either side of the cleft, and realized, perhaps for the first time, what skill, confidence and courage he was displaying. As she paid out the rope, she began to worry about him somewhere up there, in the rain, high above her, moving unprotected on wet rock. She worried for herself, as well – for she was sure that there was no way she would be able to hold him if he fell. Think of his weight. Think of the speed. Think of something else!

She thought back to the protective way he had covered her in the cleft, and was reminded of their lovemaking. The smell of him after exertion. Not sour-sweaty, but sweet: alluringly sweet. And the warmth of his breath as he came in close, prickling the back of her neck, arousing her. She suddenly realized how much she loved him, how much she needed him. She had made him suffer – *and serve him right* – but she had to be careful not to overplay her hand. A show of forgiveness was perhaps called for. Yes, she could forgive him now; she was almost sure she could. And they could start again. The next few days would be an ideal opportunity. No complications. Just the two of them. Working things out against a beautiful, wild, impartial backdrop. He had been right, suggesting this climbing expedition.

6

"Works wonders," she had so often heard him proclaim, "the magic of the outdoors." She could only hope he was right.

By the time it was her turn to climb the penultimate pitch, the rain had stopped and the sky had brightened. Soon the sun would shine again. She could see it, pale at the moment, coyly veiled in cloud, ready to burn its way through the diaphanous vapour. She was so relieved. The cleft had opened out onto a vertical wall, and the holds above her looked thin. Non-existent, some of them, till she got up close. It was scary stuff, even on a tight rope. She daren't look down. Once again she thought of what it must take to do this without a rope.

The stance she came onto was thankfully quite broad – wide enough to take three or four people – so, once she was safely clipped into the belay system, she was able to relax and take in the view.

What a difference half an hour could make in the mountains. Rain over. Sun shining warmly. A cerulean sky. Colour brought out in everything once more. Rock, drying fast. Steam rising from it. Birds, on the wing again. And from her very own eyrie she could look out across three valleys, several lakes and countless summits to the shimmering bay beyond. She could also admire Peter's broad, tanned back as he ran the rope through in readiness for the final pitch. She smiled. He never missed an opportunity to 'catch a few rays', as he put it. Yes, the world was indeed a bright and wonderful place.

"Right, ready for Toby's Jugs?" he grinned.

"For what?" she asked. "I don't . . ."

"You'll see," he twinkled, adjusting his chalk bag. "The guy who did the first ascent of this climb was called Toby Fitzpatrick. Didn't I tell you? Had a right mare of a trip. First he dislocated a finger on the second pitch. His own fault: his ring got caught on a spike of rock. Hadn't taped it over, you see. Careless, that. I always take mine off."

"Really," she said, looking relieved. It hadn't escaped her notice that he wasn't wearing his wedding ring.

7

"Yes," he said, touching his throat. "Wear it threaded on my neckband. Hadn't you noticed? Safer there. Anyway, back to poor Toby – there was far worse to come. Lost a contact lens just below the crux move – roughly where we are now. Had to more or less feel his way up the last few feet. Like a blind man reading Braille. Thought I'd told you?" He grinned. "That's why the climb's called *Blind Man's Buff* – and why that spot up there's called *Pugh Corner*."

She didn't get it at first – then she remembered her 'Treasure Island'. "Oh, how men loved these stories," she thought. "All part of the appeal. That – and all the kit. And dreaming up names for routes. Like little boys, they were. But it was endearing in a way." She suddenly felt an urge to reach out and touch him. But he had checked his harness and was already off, moving economically, gracefully, towards the narrow chimney beneath the overhang, climbing the thirty or forty feet in not many more seconds. It was lovely to watch. A combination of agility, speed, strength and technique: choreographed dance in the vertical plane.

He paused briefly in the chimney, gathering himself for the crux move. The overhang may have been 'slight' (his word), but it looked impossible to her. After a moment or two's mental rehearsal, he was on the move again – reaching up with his left hand, then with his right foot; then quickly straightening that leg to give him the height required for the next move, which took his right hand up and over the overhang. Finally, his left leg went up and straightened, enabling his left hand also to disappear from view. And suddenly he had gone.

She needed a tight rope when it was her turn – and that was before she reached the overhang. She couldn't see him, but he was above her now, ready to talk her through the crux. Once you had got your body high enough, it seemed that an act of faith was called for when the time came to reach up and over the overhang.

"Reach up and over," he called down, "and your right hand will find a knob of rock. There's another alongside it, waiting for your left hand.

8

Then, just pull on those lovely jugs . . ." she could hear him chuckling: honestly, climbers – sex mad! ". . . and you've cracked it."

Well, not quite, in her case. She felt secure enough hanging on to the jugs, but she just didn't have the strength to heave herself up to clear the overhang and he had to assist by pulling hard on the rope. Never mind. She wasn't proud. She had made it – even though, aided by that final heave on the rope, she knew she must have been dumped on the ledge like a beached whale.

They had 'topped out', as he put it, onto the broad plateau that formed the summit. It was now safe to unclip and step out of the harness that had been chafing her thighs for the last two or three hours.

"Well done!" he cried. "Knew you would do it. Not easy, either, with the weather acting up like that."

"Yes," she said, "but I couldn't have managed without you." Her eyes were shining. She felt exhilarated. "Thanks, Pete – you were – well, you were great."

She stepped forward to touch his hands, but he went straight for the bear hug. To her surprise, she didn't protest, didn't withdraw. Perhaps now was time to end it? The time to forgive and forget? The time to start a new chapter? Everything suggested that she hadn't lost him after all.

"Enjoying this now, aren't you?" he smiled.

"Yes," she said. "Never thought I would. But now I feel like staying here forever. You know – freezing the moment?" She put a hand on his wrist. "We are going to be all right, aren't we, Pete?"

"Of course," he said. "What a bloody idiot I've been. To think, I nearly lost you. Nearly lost my lovely girl, my sweetheart. I must have been insane."

They embraced, laughing through their tears.

"Tell you what," he said suddenly, breaking away but reaching for her hands, "how would you like to see how real climbers get down?"

9

"You mean, abseiling?"

"Yes, that's it," he said, his eyes shining. "Only down to that ledge we've just left. Not far. Just a taster."

"Not likely!" she said. "That last one was a really hard pitch. My limit, I'm afraid. I've had enough excitement for one day. Go down there – and I've only got to come back up again."

"That's true," he said. "But abseiling's great fun. And it's dead safe. You'd enjoy it."

"Fun for you maybe," she replied. "But you have a play if you like. I'll just watch – watch and admire."

"Okay, no pressure," he said, picking up the rope. "But you might change your mind when you see how simple it is." He grinned that boyish grin of his. "It's as simple as, well, falling off a cliff, really!"

Setting up the belay didn't take long. It was rigged in a couple of minutes. She was impressed. He beamed at her as he fiddled with something shiny in the rope system. A *descendeur*, he said it was. It cut out any rope friction, apparently, but she hadn't really listened to the technicalities. Her thoughts were elsewhere: on him, on them – on their future, their togetherness. She accompanied him as he walked towards the edge.

"Do be careful," she said. She felt a sudden shiver and reached out to touch his bare arm.

But she was too late to feel the warmth of his skin. Feet shoulder-width apart, he had jumped backwards into space and was gone.

THE DISFIGUREMENT

"Come and see me when you're ready, okay?"

As her voice sang out, I turned my head towards my bedroom door. I was just in time to catch sight of her as she skipped girlishly along the narrow hall to her room.

We had occupied our own rooms, never mind separate beds, for several years now. Not because our passion for one another had dried up. Far from it. We often made love with an intensity that our grown-up children would have thought improbable. Obscene, even.

It just seemed sensible, that's all. I like to sleep on my back, my arms and legs thrown wide apart, like a starfish, whereas she preferred to sleep on her side, knees curled up. The opposite, almost. More like a mollusc. I sometimes snore, too. You tend to, I think, when you sleep on your back. She, on the other hand, slept quiet and still as a mouse all night. Or so she liked to think.

"And don't be too long!" she added.

"Yes, Mrs Ogmore-Pritchard!" I smiled as I unbuttoned the pyjama jacket I had just put on. 'Under Milk Wood' was a great favourite of ours. "Just finishing my little tasks, my love – in order, if you please! Just closing the drawer marked pyjamas. Be with you in a minute."

I always appreciated it when she declared her need like that. It told me she was ready. Spared me any embarrassment. Not that I was generally insensitive in these matters. I know I wasn't. Most of the time, anyway. But there were occasions, especially during the early years of our marriage, when I clumsily misread the signals. It happens to most men, I assume. So it was good to be given a clear, unequivocal message. It was good to know that she was as eager as I was.

11

However, on this occasion she had soared above mere eagerness. It was almost as if she knew.

"God, you're an animal, Jenny Wyndham!" I joked, when eventually I came up for air. "A ravening animal!"

Coming out of my bedroom the next morning, I turned off the hall to go to the lavatory. I was still dazed from sleep as I pushed lightly against the door. It didn't immediately open.

"Sorry, Jen," I called, veering off towards the kitchen to put the kettle on. "Didn't realize you were up, love. Back in a few minutes with the tea."

There was no answer. All was quiet. But by then I had almost moved out of earshot.

I liked the quiet. Liked those first few minutes of the day. Just me and the purring kettle. And the view across the valley.

When I went along the hall with the teas a short time later, the lavatory door was still closed. I pushed it with my foot. When it didn't give, I felt a slight twinge of unease. But I wasn't concerned. There was sure to be a simple explanation.

I put the cups down on the carpet and pushed against the door with my hands. It resisted the pressure. Now I felt a sudden flicker of concern. It wasn't locked! There was some give in the upper half of it. Not much. Just an inch or so. Very little lower down, though. And practically none at all at floor level. Something was blocking it on the inside. Something – and now I felt a stab of fear – was preventing the door from opening. My heart started thumping. It seemed to be beating inside my head. Banging against my ear drums. Sounding like waves hitting a shelf of shingle. I heard myself cry out - a strange cry, caught in the dryness of my throat.

I lunged at the door with my shoulder. It opened a couple of inches, perhaps. No more. Then it sprang back again. It was well and truly jammed. Now I really panicked.

12

I ran round to the lavatory window at the side of the cottage.

"Jen! Jen!" I called, again and again, as I banged on the window. "Jen, can you hear me?" I was still in my pyjamas, and my bare feet, chilled by the concrete, were aching. "Jen, are you all right?"

It was a silly question. I knew she wasn't.

"Answer me, Jen, if you can," I croaked. But by now I was sure that she couldn't.

I banged repeatedly on the window, and between thumps I pressed my face close to the glass. Cupping my hands round my eyes, I tried to see inside. It was hopeless. The special glass distorted everything. In desperation, I made several attempts – several farcical attempts – to break the glass with my elbow, before giving up and running round to the garage for a hammer. Despite the cold, I was lathered in sweat.

On the way back, blinded by tears, I collided with the dustbin and fell heavily, tearing my pyjamas and grazing my knee. I cursed loudly as I got awkwardly to my feet, using the wall for support. Surprisingly, I felt no hurt. By now, I could feel nothing. Nothing but fear. Fear and panic. And, already, a sickening sense of loss.

Almost before I smashed the glass, I think I knew it was all over. I knew, even before I saw her bottom-up body slumped grotesquely against the door, that I had lost her. From the dark, empty depths of my stomach, I just knew.

Even so, I was frantic to get to her. I tried pulling myself up and onto the window ledge, but it was too high. Desperate though I was, I just didn't have the strength. All I did was cut myself on a splinter of glass.

"Shit!" I cried, as I realized I would need the step-ladders. "Oh, shit!"

Another trip to the garage. More delay.

I found myself running again. Breathing with difficulty this time. But I had to get to her quickly. Not to see if she was still alive: somehow I was sure she wasn't. But to do something about her naked bottom.

That was my first priority. As soon as I got back with the ladders, and was able to step over the glass-strewn sill and down onto the lavatory seat, that was my first, my only, thought. I had to attend to that bare, unwiped bottom.

It was not so much that it offended my sensibilities, though to my surprise, it did; but rather that I knew it would have offended hers. Even in death (and she was dead, I was sure of that) I knew she had to be relieved of that indignity as quickly as possible. She would have hated anyone to see her in that condition. Oddly, me in particular.

Afterwards. Some time afterwards. Once I had recovered from the initial shock. I tried to work out what might have happened. It wasn't easy. My distress was still acute. The whole thing was to become a recurring nightmare for me.

One thing seemed certain: death had come without any warning. Even as I stepped down from the lavatory seat, trying to avoid the mess of faeces and broken glass, that much was obvious. Caught in the middle of her toilet, she must have pitched forwards suddenly, her feet touching the floor to act as the fulcrum for a turning movement. But for the door, she would probably have turned a somersault. As it was, she had come to rest with her backside uppermost and her nightie in folds around her twisted trunk below.

Poor Jenny! I found it difficult to imagine her in a more undignified position. Her naked buttocks and thighs, rounded and enlarged by her unnatural posture, seemed to dominate the small space. I hated to see her like that. Body hideously deformed. Surrounded by mess. And that awful, unforgettable smell hanging in the air. Presiding, almost. She had always been so fastidious. Suddenly I felt sick, violently sick. Yet I didn't vomit. Nothing to bring up, I suppose.

As I wiped her bottom clean with a ball of toilet paper pulled from the roll, I guessed she had been dead for some time. Several hours, as far as I could judge. For one thing, her flesh felt cold and unnaturally

14

firm. For another, her faeces had hardened and stuck to her body. To remove it, I had to wet the paper under the tap and soak her skin.

I still hadn't seen her face. Pushed up against the door, it was partially screened by her left forearm which looked as if it could have been thrown up for protection in a sort of reflex action. It was difficult to work it out, because her body parts were all out of position somehow. Nothing seemed to be where you might expect to find it. It was bizarre. I presumed it was the way her body had settled itself after cannoning into the door.

Two things now seemed important to me. Firstly, I had to try to straighten her out. Then I had to somehow drag her backwards towards the pedestal, so that I could get the lavatory door open and move her out into the hall. Only when I had done all this, when finally she lay across my outstretched body, her head cushioned in the crook of my arm – only at that point could I bring myself to look at her face.

"Jen," I heard myself croaking. "Oh, Jenny, my love, where are you?"

I was still panting from my exertions, and a mixture of sweat and tears dripped from my chin onto her long, white neck.

"Where have you gone?" She was scarcely recognizable to me. I heard the despair rising in my voice. "Please, Jen, where have you gone?"

Listening to myself going on like that, I felt embarrassed. Ashamed, almost. But try as I did – and I did try desperately hard – I could find little resemblance between the lifeless body I held in my arms and the woman I had embraced so passionately a few hours earlier. In fact, and it broke me, filled me with shame to admit it, I found her corpse repellant.

It wasn't so much the physical disfigurement. I had been confronted with far worse in my life. No, it was something else. Something I couldn't describe adequately – until the phrase, 'the disfigurement which is death itself', came into my mind. From where?

15

C.S. Lewis, perhaps? Somebody like that. Anyway, it rang a bell. Nothing in life quite matched, quite prepared you for, that hideous disfigurement. Nothing could help you deal with the cold, flat, ugliness of death.

"I can leave that with you, then?"

I could hear someone saying this. The voice was distant, detached, dispassionate. Not mine, surely? No, it couldn't be mine. Yet I had heard it before. And wasn't that my hand holding the phone?

No, impossible! A crossed line, then? Of course! This was some fellow, sounding very matter-of-fact, very business-like, who appeared to be ringing the Council. The refuse collection department, from what I could gather. Arranging to have something taken away. Some unwanted domestic item, by the sound of it.

"Good. Oh, that's kind. I'm sorry to inconvenience you. I'll wait in then, shall I? Till you call? Okay. Goodbye."

It was my hand that put the phone down. A hand like mine, anyway. A hand with a liver spot just below the middle knuckle.

Ah, well! I made my way along the hall to the bathroom. For what purpose, I don't think I could have told you. To pee, presumably.

And suddenly, there she was. In my path. Her body. Laid out on the carpet. Blocking my way.

The sight of her did not disturb me. How strange that was! In fact, I simply stepped round her. Avoiding her. As one might, for the moment, avoid an item that would need tidying away later.

THE PHOTOGRAPH

I noticed it the first time I visited Mr. Sedgefield.

I didn't mention it, of course. I sensed it could be delicate. It needed the right moment, and that morning I was running seriously late. I didn't have a moment to spare, never mind the luxury of selecting the right one.

It was an all too familiar story. Visiting schedules rarely went to plan. Too many variables. Catch-up was a game I played every day. And I was used to losing. One look at my patient's legs told me I would be losing again.

Mr. Sedgefield's leg ulcers were the worst I had seen for some time. They were as big as two-pence pieces, and deep enough, one of them, to cover a pound coin. As I applied the dressings, I chided him for leaving it so long.

"Sorry, my dear," he said, his voice sounding genuinely apologetic. "Didn't want to trouble you. Know how busy you all are." He paused and fixed me with a rheumy eye. "Also, to be honest, I worry about calling people in. Somebody's going to come along one of these days and say I'm a liability. 'Too much of a risk to be left on his own,' they're going to say. That's my big fear – losing my independence."

"Well, you will if you start neglecting yourself like this," I smiled, wagging a warning finger at him. "They were very weepy. Caught them just in time. Apart from the ulcers, though, you seem to be coping quite well."

And he was. I saw from his notes that he'd had a pretty rough time of it in the last four years: bowel cancer operation, followed by months of chemo-therapy – and then, just as he was recovering, a thrombosis. At about the same time, just for good measure, he had begun to have trouble with cataracts. Life can be tough sometimes; I'm often reminded. But, despite everything – and particularly once the laser treatment had restored his sight, so that he could go back to his books – he had picked himself up and got on with life's journey. Sure, he had poor circulation in his legs, and he was finding it increasingly difficult to get about; but he was doing all right.

"Yes, I manage just fine." He smoothed down his sparse, thin hair. I noticed for the first time that he was wearing a hearing aid. "Things will keep dropping off me, of course." he smiled. "But by now I'm used to that."

I looked around. Yes, he had certainly got himself organized. He'd had the downstairs of the house adapted so that everywhere was on one level, down to the big walk-in shower space. 'In what used to be the kitchen,' he told me. The living room was perhaps a bit cramped; but everything was to hand, including a specially created kitchen/utility area, fully equipped. All surfaces clean and tidy, too. I was impressed.

"What's behind the curtain, Mr. Sedgefield?" I asked, as I was packing my bag to leave. I saw his face. "Sorry, I'm being nosy, aren't I?"

"No, not at all," he said. "You're keeping an inspectorial eye on me. Part of your job. No – don't deny it!" He looked at me knowingly. "Anyway, I'll let you see." He smiled and his watery eyes twinkled. He was well past his sell-by date, of course, but I thought what a charmer he must have been in his day. "If you'll promise to call me George."

"Agreed, George," I laughed. "But only if you promise to call me June."

He got unsteadily to his feet, waving away my gesture of help, and walked on his sticks to the alcove.

"Voila!" he cried, pulling back the curtain theatrically to reveal a shiny new computer station. "You see before you, courtesy of my daughter, an old man dragged whimpering into the twenty-first

18

century!" He laughed. "Well, not quite. I've revived some research I once started – and it's invaluable, this little chappy." He moved a liver-spotted hand, caressingly almost, over the contours of the sleek machine. "For chasing up references, ordering books: that kind of thing."

"Well, good for you, George," I said. "I'm impressed. And I can't wait to hear more. But I'll have to love you and leave you, I'm afraid. I'm over forty minutes late as it is. So, see you tomorrow – okay? And do be careful, moving about. Take your time. Try not to knock your legs on things. That's how they start, you know – ulcers."

It was then, as I was leaving, that I saw it on the sideboard. Turned to the wall. This was what intrigued me. Everywhere else was meticulously orderly. A place for everything, and everything in its place: that seemed to be George's motto. Except for this photograph. Why was it turned to the wall, I wondered?

The next morning, I looked for it especially. It was still facing the wall. Fascinating! If I had time in hand later, I determined, I would choose my moment to ask about it.

"Looks out for you, then, your daughter?" I nodded in the direction of the alcove as I started to change the dressings. "You know – the computer?"

"Ah, yes. All the alterations are down to her as well. She's a good girl, my Pauline. Well, not so much a girl now. Forty-five, she is. A consultant in Reading. Always kept very busy. But never too busy to keep an eye on her old dad. Comes up at least once a month, she does. You know – checking up on me."

Ah, the wily old devil! Yes, he was on to me, all right. He knew I was taking everything in. I could tell from his tone.

"I don't mind, though," he went on, twinkling his eyes in that winsome way he had. "We're very close. Both like a drop of gin, for one thing. And a good red. I look forward to her visits."

"That's marvellous," I said. "You're very lucky to have such a daughter." I looked across at the sideboard. "You haven't got a photo of her, by any chance?"

"Sorry, I didn't catch . . ." he said, putting a finger to his hearing aid. But he had followed my eyes. "Ah, the . . . I see. Yes, I have photos – but that's not Pauline. That's my wife." He saw my expression and grinned nervously. "And, oh dear, she seems to have turned her back on us." He paused, looking a little uncomfortable. "All right, I know!" he surrendered. "It must seem a bit odd. If you must know, I, and you're going to think this very silly of me, I don't like her looking at me." He looked down at his bloated, disfigured legs. "It's daft, of course – quite irrational – but she'd be very upset, seeing me like this." He laughed. "Dear me – you must think I'm losing my marbles."

"Not at all," I said, offering what I hoped was a reassuring smile. Actually, I found the notion very amusing. Also, in a way, quite touching. I began to apply the new dressings.

"Yes, that's Margaret," he said, trying to regain his composure. "As was, anyway. Died twelve years ago. She was a beautiful woman. Lovely nature, too. Thirty-six wonderful years, we had. My best friend and sweetheart. Right through to the end. I'm sorry: that must sound awfully twee, but it's true." His eyes began to fill, and he turned his head away. "A bugger, isn't it?" He spoke with some difficulty, unable to look at me. "Cancer, I mean. . . That's why she's specializing in it, I reckon. My daughter, that is." He paused, seeking to change tack. "She's very like her mother. I'll show you next time. Everyone remarks on it. And she has that same. . . " His voice trailed away.

"Time to leave," I thought.

When I tapped on the door the following morning, there was no answer. I didn't think it strange. My first appointment had been cancelled: I was nearly half-an-hour early.

I tried the door. It was not locked.

20

"Coo-ee," I called, as I entered. "George – it's me, June, the District Nurse. Are you there?"

From the shower area I could hear the noise of falling water. George was obviously making himself presentable for my visit. Such a fastidious man. I turned towards the sideboard, intending to take a look at the photograph of his wife, but a flicker of light from the opposite side of the room distracted me. The curtain was pulled back and the computer was still on. I walked over, my curiosity getting the better of me. Now, what was this research of his all about?

Even as I approached, I knew I was about to see something I wasn't meant to see. The sound alone should have given it away. Animal noises: that was my first thought. Some nature programme, perhaps? But I quickly realized that they were the sort of noises people make when they're making love. Losing control sort of noises. Then, as I reached the flickering machine, I saw the bodies. And not just two bodies. Not just a man and a woman. There were four of them – one man and three women. Writhing about, they were, their naked bodies twisted into impossible positions. And the disgusting things they were doing to one another! It was nauseating.

My first impulse was to stand my ground – to remain there, in front of the screen, ready to confront him when he came through from the shower. I suppose I wanted to shame him. I'm no prude, but I can't stand that sort of filth.

Then I thought – no, steady on, girl: you're a professional, remember. Not your place to be judgmental. Forget your own feelings; think of the patient.

I managed to pull myself up short. After all, where was the harm? He was just a man – and an old man at that – who was feeling an itch and needed to scratch it. That's all it was, surely? It wasn't as if he was into child pornography. That would have been different. No: it was quite harmless, in a way. And all done in the privacy of his own home.

21

A privacy I had invaded. Accidentally, it was true – but I shouldn't have been so nosy.

So I tiptoed quietly out of the room, out of the house, and made myself scarce in the local park for half-an-hour. As I strolled between the flowerbeds, my mood was sad. Silly, I know, but I felt let down somehow. I wanted to put the clock back, pretend I hadn't blundered in like that.

George greeted me cheerfully, as usual.

"Come in, come in," he said. "I have Margaret and Pauline here," his eyes twinkled "ready to meet you!"

He led the way into the living room and stopped in front of the sideboard, on which there now stood two framed photographs. I studied them for several seconds. He was right: his wife was beautiful. And so was his daughter, smiling alongside her. They could have been sisters, I thought.

"Well, now you've met my family, I suppose we'd better get on," he said, turning his wife's photograph to face the wall again. We exchanged glances. "Sorry – like I say, I don't like to think of her looking at me. Seeing me like this. Seeing what I've come to. It would upset her." He paused. "You do understand, don't you?"

His mouth attempted a brave, open smile; but I was concentrating on his eyes. The skin around them puckered, but for me they no longer twinkled. I thought I could now detect a certain shiftiness.

"Of course," I said. "Self-image, and all that. So important. I understand you perfectly."

I opened my bag and took out the dressings.

"Now, Mister Sedgefield – let's get down to business, shall we?"

My voice was cool, my manner brusque. Not my usual style. I felt a little ashamed of myself.

THE DISCOVERERS

"What are we looking for, Grandad?"

"Treasure."

"Treasure! What – you mean like gold and diamonds, and things?"

"Not quite," laughed the old man, a little out of breath as they made their way, hand in hand, down the cliff path. "Wouldn't cost much in the shops. But worth more. In my book, any road."

"I don't understand," said the boy. "If they don't cost much, how can they . . .? What sort of things?"

"Oh, I don't know. Anything, really." It was hard, the old man thought, to explain some things. Small boys wanted a ready answer. It wasn't always as simple as that. "Anything unusual, I suppose. Anything that makes your heart leap. Aye, that's it."

"Hearts can't leap, Grandad!" The boy chuckled; the image had clearly amused him. "How can they leap? They've got no legs!"

"Nor have salmon – and they leap."

A long silence followed. The boy had to think about that one.

They reached the foot of the cliff and found a flat rock on which to leave their bait and their waterproofs. "Base camp", the old man called it, and that gave rise to more questions. Thankfully, they were much easier to answer than the earlier ones.

Heads down, absorbed, man and boy began to quarter the beach. They were often ten or more yards apart during the search, but the thread of intimacy that connected them was never broken. They worked quietly, the silence broken only by the distant breaking of waves, the mewing of gulls and the periodic cries of pleasure as little 'finds' were placed carefully in the plastic pail.

23

Two hours passed. It seemed more like two minutes. So engrossed were they that neither of them thought of food – not even the thick, hot soup waiting for them in the old man's battered vacuum flask back at base camp.

"Wow!" cried the boy, suddenly. "Look at this, Grandad."

"Hey, that's great! Well done," enthused his grandfather. "How lucky is that. It's an ammonite. Big one, too. Wait till your Mam and Dad see that!"

Eyes shining, the two companions examined the spiraled wonder more closely. Its local name, 'St. Hilda's Serpent', didn't need much explaining. The boy was able to trace its outline with his finger as his grandfather told him the legend of the Abbess of Whitby.

"Imagine that! Just one look from the Abbess, that's all it took." The old man concluded. "And that hissing, coiled snake was turned to stone!"

The boy's eyes were as big as saucers. He told a good tale, did his Grandad.

On the way back up the cliff, the boy put his free hand into his grandfather's big palm. He liked the squeeze it was given: strong, yet gentle. His other hand held a piece of treasure that hadn't seen the light of day for over two hundred million years. Now it was locked away again in his privileged fingers.

"Grandad?"

"Yes?"

"Know what?"

"No – what?"

"Know what? Back there, on the beach." His eyes were shining like precious stones. "I think my heart was a salmon!"

24

THE TRIBUTE

"A tricky one, that," said the one called Kevin. "Very hard to say, till we take a look."

He was about her age, she guessed, with thinning fair hair and a large, aquiline nose. His mate – a gangly youth with a nervous, anxious-to-please smile – was much younger, probably no more than eighteen or nineteen.

"But I should warn you before we start," went on Kevin, blinking in the morning sunshine before taking a sip of tea and then reaching for another half-chocolate digestive, "they won't be hurried, your drains. Usually turn out to be long jobs. Am I right, Titch?"

"Aye," smiled Titch, "you can't hurry drains."

"In that case," she said, regretting already her offer of tea before they had even begun, "I'd better let you make a start."

"You're right. We'd best be cracking on," said Kevin. "So drink up, lad, and get that manhole cover lifted. Be with you in a tick."

He drained his mug slowly, before leaning back on the legs of the garden chair and smacking his lips audibly.

"Good cuppa, that, missus. Thanks." He looked appreciatively along the lawn to the low wall and the fields beyond. "Grand out here, eh. Just you and Mother Nature." He looked from her to the fields again, this time tilting his head back slightly to take in the line of the pastel-blue ridge that leapt gracefully across the distant skyline. "Aye," he sighed. "My idea of heaven, that."

"Yes, it is nice," she said, collecting the tea things onto a tray. "But I must get on. I'll be around if you need me."

She returned to her kitchen and set about the washing-up. As she transferred the dishes to the drying rack, she smiled ruefully. 'They won't be hurried, your drains!'

Ten minutes later, Kevin was back with the news that there was no blockage where the drain emptied into the sewer, which meant that the water she had noticed welling up from the lawn wasn't caused by what he referred to as a *wash-back*.

"It's just as I suspected," he said. "There's a blockage further up. Like, under your lawn. Either that, or your drainage pipes are knackered! And that's a possibility, I'm afraid. All this used to be agricultural land, see. Before it was sold for building, like. I remember it as a lad. So they could be yonks old, some of these pipes. We won't know, though, till we get the rods on the job."

"The what?"

"The rods," he repeated. He smiled indulgently. "You know, like the ones chimley sweeps used in the olden days? To push up your flue, like."

"But how can rods tell if there's a blockage?' she asked, trying to ignore what she took to be an obvious *double-entendre*.

"Ah," he replied, tapping his temple, "we're not just common navvies these days, you know." He sucked in his thin lips. "Oh, no! Thanks to modern technology, we're more like drain surgeons, you might say." He laughed at his little joke, before going on. "We stick a tiny camera on the end of the first rod, see. Then we can look at the screen and suss the problem. Get me?"

"Completely," she said, rather curtly. It irritated her when people – men, usually – patronized her in this fashion. *What was there to get, for Christ's sake!* Then she relented. You couldn't really blame him for trying to talk up what was surely little more than manual labour. "Yes, very clever. The wonders of modern science, eh?"

26

"Exactly!" he cried, seemingly delighted. The chance to share one of the secrets of his trade didn't come often, perhaps. "Back in a tick with the result."

In fact, it was half an hour before she heard him knock again. *Trouble with the technology?* she wondered.

"Just as I suspected!" he said triumphantly when she opened the door. "No blockage. Your pipes have disintegrated. Knackered, they are! Just how knackered, well, we won't know till we open him up, like."

"Sorry?" she queried, wondering if she had heard correctly.

"You know – dig into your lawn. Make an incision." He laughed. "Drain surgeons – remember?" He paused, perhaps expecting her to laugh at his little joke. "Yes, well, that all right then?" he went on, trying to read her reluctant smile. "Don't worry, we'll be careful. When we sew him up again, that is. You know, when we put the turfs back? A couple of weeks and you won't know we've been here. You'll hardly see the scar, I promise."

She didn't manage any sort of smile this time. Just a sniff. She knew she ought to be making more of an effort. It wasn't his fault, after all. He wasn't to know. Too soon, that was all.

"I need your permission, though," he continued, for the first time sounding unsure of himself. "Before we proceed, like."

"Permission?" Her eyes were open, but they appeared unseeing; and her voice had wandered off somewhere. "My consent? Yes, of course. If that's what it takes, you must do it." Her tone – so cold, so detached – suddenly disturbed her. The voice seemed remote, the sound of it not of her making somehow. "Yes, just get on with it. It's only a bit of grass, for Christ's sake!"

"Yes, well, we have to ask," he said. "And it's such a nice lawn." He was clearly a little stung by her abruptness. "Before we start, though, do you think I could use your toilet? I'll take my boots off."

27

Five minutes later, she came through from the front of the house to see if there was any chance that he might actually be making a start. She found him sitting on the step, pulling his boots on.

"That photo?" he said, hearing her approach and half-turning.

"Sorry?"

"You know, the one on the table outside the toilet? The one in the silver frame?"

"Yes – my father?" she shot him a quizzical look. *Such impertinence!* she thought. When was the man going to get down to some work?

"Mr Todd, right?"

"Yes, that's Leslie Todd," she began, a note of suspicion creeping into her voice, "but how...?"

"Well, would you believe it?" he beamed. "Your dad – *The Sweeney!*" She now looked totally baffled. "Ah, sorry – that's what we called him: '*The Sweeney*'. You know: Sweeney Todd – Flying Squad. On the telly. All the rage then, it was."

"Oh, yes," she said, "very droll."

"Not if you were in Tennyson, it wasn't. Your dad was our housemaster, see. And if you were up to no good you didn't stand a bloody earthly – not with the Sweeney on your case, you didn't. Good bloke, though. Firm, but fair. Know what I mean? Good teacher, an' all."

"So I understand," she said. She swallowed hard. "He was a good dad, too."

"Yes, I'm sorry. A great loss." he said. "Saw it in the paper. Even thought about going. You know, to the funeral? To pay my respects, like."

"That's well, thank you for the thought. Very kind." Through the tremor, her voice now sounded warmer, more welcoming. "You wouldn't have been alone. There were scores of former pupils there. A

28

really big congregation, it was. So many people! Complete strangers came up to me, offering their remembrances. I was touched. *Treasured memories*, some said." She paused and drew a deep breath. "I knew he was popular, of course. But I never realized just . . . But then, he was at Boddington all his teaching life. Taught most of the pupils' parents. One or two grandparents, even. Part of the bricks and mortar, people said."

"Yes, well – like I say," Kevin said, "I'm very sorry." Then suddenly he brightened. "I seem to remember he was very keen on the apostrophe, your dad."

"I'll say!" she said. *'The Apostropher Royal'*, we called him. You weren't alone; we all suffered, I'm afraid."

"Yes," he continued. "Always on about it, he was. *'The comma in the air'*, I believe he called it. I can hear him now. *'Make sure, my friends, that you put it in its place',* he used to say. Being thick, though, I never could work out where the bugger was supposed to live – if you'll pardon the language! And to this day it still has its way with me, the apostrophe. I've never really got topside of it."

"I wouldn't let it worry you," she smiled. "There are more important things. . ." Her face turned serious again. "Anyway, I must get on. My daughter will be back soon. Never done, is it – a body's work?"

"Too right," he said. "Got to crack on myself. And don't you worry. I'll make sure the job's a good-un." He walked away shaking his head. "Would you believe it – *The Sweeney*'s daughter!"

Four hours and three trays of tea later, she looked out of the sitting room window and peered along the avenue. Late again! What was it with musicians? Professionally, time was crucial; they were slaves to it. But in their private lives, they let it do as it pleased. Kevin's apostrophe came suddenly to mind, and the image amused her.

29

She wasn't worried for Karen's safety. Alan was a good dad; she had never been reluctant to acknowledge that. He'd been a good husband, too, in many ways. Two years on, she could concede that as well. There had been a lot of love, for sure. Such a shame he'd felt the urge to share his portion around so generously. His cavalier attitude to time, though: that still irritated her.

It was the same with regard to the rest of his life. No self-discipline. Like a child, he was. Just couldn't see beyond the moment, couldn't project, couldn't see the possible consequences of his actions. Any moment now – or, more likely, at some point in the next hour or so! – he would stop his car at the end of the avenue as usual, give Karen a kiss and one of his big, friendly bear hugs, and then be on his way, quite oblivious of the fact that he was hours late, that food might be spoiling.

She returned to her kitchen to remove a pie from the oven. Then, shedding her oven gloves, she turned to the window. The trench was about three metres long now, with neat, straight sides dropping down into deep shadow. She could see no sign of piping: just the broad, dark scar across the lawn – and, to the side, on a carefully placed sheet of plastic, two piles, one of stones, the other, much larger, of soil. The image made her shudder. Her father's incision had left a long, red scar zipping down from navel to pubis. *A neat bit of sewing*, the registrar had laughed. But his skill with the needle had been in vain: the cancer had already spread. She turned away, dabbing her eyes quickly with her apron.

There was a light tap on the back door. *Not again! That man and his tea!* But she smiled. She was starting to change her view of Kevin; there was more to him than met the eye. And he was proving to be a good worker.

"Sorry to disturb you," Kevin began. He was holding something to his chest, carefully – tenderly, almost – as if it were a baby. "Only I thought you ought to see this before your little girl comes in. Not too late, am I?"

"No, she's not back yet," she said, hearing a tinge of resentment in her voice. She looked closely at the soil-encrusted object. It appeared to be some sort of container, but so old, so decomposed, that it seemed to be falling apart. "What on earth . . .?" she began. Then she managed a nervous laugh. "I say – not buried treasure, is it?"

"No," he smiled, "though it could've been once, you might say." He began to pull away the crumbling lid. "It's hard to say now what it is – or *was*. Puppy, maybe? Difficult to tell. Not much left of it, I'm afraid." He straightened his arms to let her examine it. "Something small, anyway."

"Oh, dear," she cried, stepping back, "the poor thing! Yes, thank you. I believe I know. . . " she faltered. "My daughter. . . she must have. . ."

"Thought you'd know," he said. "And I guessed it had to be some sort of pet." He bent down and put the box, or whatever it was, gently, almost reverently, onto the ground. Despite his care, parts of it flaked off and soiled the path. "And I thought it might upset the little girl if – well, you know. . ."

"Yes, it was years ago, but I think it still might," she said. "She thought the world. . ." she faltered. "Thank you, it's very thoughtful of you. I think we just. . . "

"Quietly dispose of it?" he anticipated.

"Please – if you wouldn't mind."

"No problem," he said cheerily. "Leave it with me. I'm thinking of having a break now, as it happens, so I'll take it off somewhere. You know, find it a new resting place. Some quiet little spot, nice and peaceful, like."

Ten minutes later, when the two men broke for lunch, Titch went off somewhere with the van. To the nearest pub, she guessed. Kevin, however – spade in one hand, black polythene bag in the other –

31

climbed over the low wall and disappeared into the fields. Half-an-hour later, she saw him coming back across the lawn clutching a large bunch of wild flowers.

"Thought these might look nice at your kitchen window," he said. "You know – splash of colour. Cheer you up a bit." He smiled. "Call it a tribute to the little girl's animal friend. To *The Sweeney* as well."

"Thank you, Kevin," she said, feeling embarrassingly touched by his simple act. "That's very. . ."

The sound of a door closing at the front of the house rescued her. Offering her apologies, she crossed the kitchen and turned into the hall, giving her cheeks a quick dab as she moved.

"Good time, sweetheart?" she enquired, pulling Karen into the oven-like warmth of her apron.

"Yes, it was great. Yesterday, for sure. Well cool! We went to Victoria Park to see 'Alice in Wonderland'. The Mad Hatter's Tea Party was great fun. And the game of croquet, played with hedgehogs and flamingoes – pretend ones, of course – was like, well, wonderful!" Karen paused to take a breath. "We sat on the bank, with a picnic. That was yummy. We had smoked salmon, and bits of chicken tika, oh, and all kinds of things. And Angela. . ."

"Angela? Who's Angela?"

"Daddy's new girlfriend."

"Oh, no – not another one! What happened to Julie?"

"Oh, she left. Couldn't stand the trumpet, Daddy said. Anyway, Angela gave me a few sips of her wine when Daddy wasn't looking, and the bubbles went up my nose and made me sneeze! I like her, Mum. Better than Julie. We had races by the lake after the show – and you should have seen her run! Daddy came last every time, of course. He should stop smoking, you know. I've told him."

"Waste of time!" said her mother. "You know your Daddy. I tried often enough. Got tired of being called an old nag-bag!" She laughed. 'Goes with the job', she was tempted to say. 'Trumpet, fag, drink – and girl friend. All to do with gratifying the lips.' "Anyway, I'm glad you enjoyed it. Hope you're hungry, by the way. I've cooked your favourite. About half-an-hour – that all right?"

"What's going on at the back?" asked Karen, pulling a chair to the table. "Those men?"

"They're here to fix the drains," her mother explained. "That water we had bubbling up after last week's rain – and that smell!"

"Like rotten cabbage! Don't remind me."

"Yes, well, the drainage pipes under the lawn were rotten, apparently. We need new ones. The men came this morning. They'll be leaving soon. Back tomorrow with the new pipes. Plastic ones, this time."

"I see." Karen paused; she was looking thoughtful "The men, when they were digging, did they, you know, find anything?"

"No," laughed her mother. "Apart from a mountain of stones! Why do you ask?"

"Oh, nothing," said Karen.

A little later, cloth in hand, she was lending a hand with the washing up.

"Mam," she began. "Grandles was a good man, wasn't he?"

"What a question! You know he was. The best, in my book. What do you think?"

"I think he was the best granddad in the world! In fact, I think Daddy's right." Her mother looked puzzled. "Daddy thinks Grandles is *still* a good man. Even though he's no longer with us. Making fine soil, Daddy says. Still doing good."

"Well, that's Daddy talking." *What an odd thing to say to a child!* "Says some funny things sometimes."

"I think he's right, though," said Karen. "No – I *know* he's right! Today proves it." She saw her mother's face. "Well, the men out there, digging? Found nothing – yes?" Her mother, looking puzzled, nodded. "But that's where I buried Chestnut. You know, my guinea-pig."

"Yes, of course I remember Chestnut," said her mother. "He was very special, I know. But I thought. . ."

"No – when you were out shopping, that's where me and Daddy buried him. Not out in the field – but there, where the onions used to grow. You know – where we used to have the vegetable patch. And the men say he's not there anymore. So don't you see – he must have turned to soil! And Grandles is doing the same. It makes sense now."

"Yes," said her mother, reaching forward and squeezing her daughter's forearm. "It's a lovely idea."

"Bit of a mess, though – the lawn," responded Karen, suddenly changing tack. "When will it be finished?"

"Oh, not for days, I imagine," said her mother. She was feeling surprisingly relaxed. "I'm told they can be long jobs, your drains."

GRISELLE

Luke de Ville, he had called himself.

It wasn't his real name; she was convinced of that. In fact, she had gradually come to understand that very little about him was real. He was a phony. A fantasist. Not what he seemed. This was what riled her. She had long ago had enough of him and his weird ways – and now suddenly he had done to her what she should have had the pleasure of doing to him several weeks back.

She was mildly surprised how little she missed him – *good riddance, more like!* – yet she was angry. Angry with herself. He had outflanked her yet again.

They had met at a Halloween party just over a year ago. She had gone as a witch – one of seven; quite a coven – and he had gone as a Pan-like figure with a woven tail, far too long for a goat, and high-protruding ears that stuck out like horns. They had danced together at one point – a wild, frenzied fling during which, hilariously, they kept tripping over his tail – and afterwards, beneath the trees at the end of the garden, he had groped her through her witch's weeds. "Scientific curiosity," he had laughingly excused himself. "Searching for the witch's mark!" She had smacked his face rather too hard, bringing off one of his ears. This had set them giggling like a couple of kids. The next morning she had phoned the number he had cunningly stuck to her pointy hat.

He had moved in with her just before Christmas. Or rather, he had started at that time to sleep at her house almost every night – for he never really moved out of his own place. That was why he arrived with so few possessions: toiletries, a laptop, a few books with arcane titles, a spare set of clothes and a small wooden chest with a strange, inscribed symbol on the lid, always kept locked. He was quite open about keeping his flat going – his 'bolt-hole', he called it – but she was never even allowed to know *where* he lived, let alone invited to step inside to see where he stored the rest of his stuff, where all his mail was delivered – and where, from time to time, he would spend two or three nights together, 'attending to business', as he put it. What this 'business' was precisely, she never knew. "I dabble," he had once said archly, enjoying as usual the role of man of mystery. "In finance, mainly," he had added laughingly, "with a bit of alchemy on the side!" That was all she ever got out of him.

She knew next to nothing about him, when she came to think of it. He never volunteered information about himself; nor would he answer any questions directly. What scant knowledge she had of him was based entirely on her own observations. The way he dressed, for example: usually all in black, but sometimes, weirdly, almost entirely in green. And his food preferences: he was very fond of mushrooms, which in season he would go out and collect for himself, but for some reason he couldn't stand garlic – wouldn't have it in the house – which was a shame because she loved it. His taste in music – either classical (particularly Wagner and any of the baroque composers) or heavy metal – differed widely from hers, too. All pop music was trivial, in his view. He thought the same of her weakness for magazines and light fiction; he liked gothic novels and writers like Tolkien, Pullman, Peake; and he was fascinated, it seemed, by anything to do with the supernatural and the occult.

All of this she could manage, she thought. She had been around the block; she knew about compromise. So, okay – a bit of give and take was called for: no problem. But two things were destined to become intolerable. First, his obsessive tidiness. This had soon got to her – though probably, she later consoled herself, not half as much as her slap-dash ways had got to him! Second, by far the most important, his constant need to be in control – of both people and events. This had

36

not been apparent at first; but when he moved in with her, she soon came to realize what a control freak he was. He really wanted to have dominion over all aspects of her life – her friends, the way she dressed, the food she ate, the music she listened to, and so on – and she wasn't having it. Above all else, this was the thing she knew she wouldn't be able to cope with. For his part, Luke soon began to see the feisty side of her – and it was her stubborn determination to be her own woman, she supposed, that had caused him to take off suddenly, the way he had.

Well, what the hell! He was good in bed, she had to give him that. Although come to think of it, their love-making, too, had been based on his desire to dominate and her willingness to be submissive. But life wasn't just about sex – and even if it were, she had smiled, there would surely be other fish in the sea.

And there were. During the next few weeks she revelled in the many freedoms that went with living alone again, rediscovering among other things the excitement of casual sex. Yes, life was sweet. She had forgotten how much you concede when you commit yourself to another person. The monkey was off her back now; she was in charge again. She had never been happier.

Then one day, there was a surprise awaiting her on the front doorstep. And it appeared as if by magic. When Emma went to empty the mailbox, the step was bare. A little more than five minutes later, just as she was letting herself out to go to work, there the wretched creature was – demanding immediate attention, *starting as it means to go on!* – with not a soul in sight, not a clue as to where it had come from. It was as if it had been spirited down. But it couldn't be ignored. Nor could the warning Emma was to receive from her boss for being late later that morning.

Emma had never liked cats. In her view they were too self-sufficient – no, too self-absorbed: that was more accurate. And silently judgmental, she always thought, as they sat there motionless – yet

37

somehow always alert, always ready; ever watchful – staring you out. That was another thing about them: their slitty eyes. She found it really spooky, the way their pupils could change like that. And their retractable claws: yes, that was something else. Like sheathed knives: potentially deadly, but kept hidden. A bit sneaky, that! She wasn't exactly afraid of cats; but they certainly made her feel very uneasy. And to have one gifted like this – as if from nowhere, in a basket, mewling like a baby – was perverse and puzzling. And – because she couldn't just leave it there – bloody infuriating!

The cat was obviously thirsty and hungry, but as she let it out of its basket she could see that it was otherwise in good condition. Its eyes were bright and its coat – black, with a white patch, oval-shaped, on the top if its head – was shiny and in good condition. She gave it a saucer of milk and looked in her cupboard for something more substantial. At first, the creature turned its nose up at the sardines; but when nothing better was offered, it sniffed and nuzzled the fish fastidiously for a few moments – *yes, don't appear too eager, too grateful, whatever you do!* – before clearing the dish and licking it clean.

Emma made several attempts to get the cat back into the basket; she didn't want the damned thing to have the run of the house while she was at work. But it wouldn't be persuaded. Each time she cornered it and approached, it arched its back and spat at her; she found that quite intimidating. In the end she had to settle for locking it in the kitchen, knowing that she was now committing herself to a day of worry about the mess it might make. One of the girls she had shared with during her final year at Sheffield had a cat. Against the rules, probably. Sooty, it was called. Emma had never forgotten it. Particularly the pungent smell of cat shit when the students let themselves in after lectures. She had a horror of cat mess.

But her interloper, she found, when she returned home that evening, had behaved impeccably. It was lying languorously beneath the radiator – *the warmest place in the room, of course!* – on a tea towel which had been left to dry. Her college friend, Julie, would have positively purred. "Yes, they know just how far to go." Emma could almost hear her saying it. "They have this incredible, intuitive understanding; a sixth sense, if you like." *What a load of cobblers!* In Emma's view, cats were the ultimate kidologists. A bit like Luke, really. Not what they seemed. Yet you had to hand it to them: it demanded a special sort of intelligence and ingenuity for an animal with a relatively small brain to turn itself into such an accomplished free-loader. She could of course see why they were revered in some cultures, in that their aloofness and inscrutability – their very silence, indeed – could make them appear all-knowing. But she had got their number. They were nothing more than rather sinister, house-wise little creatures who had developed cunning ways of ensuring that they were always warm and well-fed, offering in return no true loyalty – they were loyal only to themselves – and a mere semblance of affection. This was what she thought; and this was why she mistrusted them. If you happened to drop dead in the act of feeding a cat, it would immediately insinuate itself with whoever took over from you. And this slinky, little number, as it brushed against her legs, was at this very moment proving her point. Furthermore, as expected, it was operating coolly, dispassionately, with unblinking eyes.

"Well," she said, addressing the cat before she went to bed, "you may be clever in a cunning, kitty-catty sort of way, but you can't tell me where you've come from, can you? And unless I get some answers by the weekend, you'll be off to the cats' home, or the glove factory, before you can say meow!"

The animal had a temporary reprieve on Thursday; there was a brief message in Emma's emails.

Have had to go away for a spell.
Know you're missing me terribly,

*but now you have Griselle to take
my place! She's rather special,
I think you'll find. Look after
one another till I return for her.
Explain everything later. Luke.*

That's all it said. Emma was livid, particularly as she had quickly dismissed an early notion that Luke might be responsible. Even he wouldn't be so crass, she had reasoned; for he knew full well how much she disliked cats. *The callous bugger! How twisted, how perverse could you get?*

Two, four, six weeks went by. Emma, perhaps predictably, had yet to hear again from Luke. Griselle, perhaps less predictably, was still keeping warm and well-nourished under Emma's roof. Emma wasn't altogether sure why this was so. Why hadn't she rid herself of her unwelcome guest on day one? Well partly, she told herself, because she couldn't act until she had received the promised explanation from Luke. Then there were pressures to do with her job. She was going through a bad patch at work, which meant the need at weekends to chill out and off-load the stress; this had left her no time to find out how one humanely disposed of an unwanted cat. And apart from all this, of course, there was no way she was going to give Luke the satisfaction of thinking badly of her. She wanted rid of the damned creature. Of course she did. She had always despised cats. But her predicament was not of the cat's making. She had to avoid acting rashly, impulsively; she had to show Luke that some people knew how to behave in a decent, civilized fashion.

This was what she told herself; but she knew they were merely excuses. The fact was that in the beginning she couldn't fault the animal's behaviour; and, reluctant though she was to admit it, she found that Giselle was company of sorts. With no man in her life at that point, Emma found that Ellie (as she had taken to calling her) was something to come home to. Okay, she couldn't have a two-way conversation with her – Emma didn't find her *that* 'special', as Luke had put it – but she found it really helpful to sound off to her about problems at work. It was better, at least, than ranting on at the cooker!

And so it was during those few weeks that one resourceful cat and its reluctant, fostering mistress went through an unlikely honeymoon period. It may have fallen well short of a natural symbiosis – in that Emma never lost her cynical view that with cats the dependency would always be somewhat one-sided – but it was, for a while, a tolerable co-existence.

The changes, when they came about, were subtle and gradual – to the point that Emma, once she became aware of what was happening to her, was amazed at how cunningly she was being manipulated.

It started, somewhat improbably, with cauliflower-cheese, one of her favourite dishes. As soon as the cheese was uncovered and the cauliflower was on the boil, Ellie began to get restless; clearly she wasn't keen on the smell. She would then become increasingly irritated, until finally she would scratch at the door to be let out. On the first couple of occasions, Emma thought it was amusing; but the fuss Ellie made, not to mention the damage she inflicted on the paint-work, began to get to her. Cauliflower-cheese was eventually taken off the menu.

Then there was Dusty Springfield. Emma had inherited from her mother a weakness for romantic ballads, and Dusty was one of her favourites. She didn't play her all the time; nothing like that. But occasionally the mood would take her – and then, as soon as Dusty's distinctive voice filled the room, Ellie would set up such a caterwauling that the music couldn't even be heard let alone appreciated.

However, it wasn't until Ellie started to take a hand in selecting her mistress's men friends that Emma declared *enough is enough!* The cat had an interesting way of involving itself in the selection process. She would crouch on top of the dresser, motionless but sprung for action, fixing the male caller with a cold, unblinking, mesmerizing stare. If need be, the technique could be taken up another notch; this saw Ellie drop effortlessly to the carpet and move gradually closer and closer to her prey, as if ready at any second to pounce. All but the boldest could be freaked out in this way. And perhaps no bad thing, Emma thought, if you were looking for a man to father fearless children – except that Ellie also seemed particularly adept at screening out handsome men and men with talent. Potential rivals, in other words. It had to stop. The creature was starting to run her life. It was the Luke situation all over again. Luke – without the sex! No, Ellie had to go, she was beginning to realize.

The very day after this thought had penetrated, a strange thing happened. She came home from work as usual, but as soon as she let herself in she was aware that something was wrong. There was no Ellie to greet her! No excited purring. No elegant wisp of warm fur threading its way in and out between her legs as she stepped into the kitchen. Nothing but a rather unsettling silence. There was a pang of disappointment; it made her realize suddenly what she would be missing.

"Ellie, I'm home," she called, as she stepped from the kitchen into the hall. "Ellie, where are you? I'm home."

But there was no sign of her. "That's strange," she thought. She checked the bedrooms. Still no sign. "Very strange!" She opened the door to the sitting room. She needed a drink.

"What the. . .!" she cried, as she stepped into the room – for there, stretched out on the sofa, large as life, glass in one hand, book in the other, was Luke!

"You look surprised, my sweet," he said. "Or are you just overwhelmed with delight!"

42

"How the hell did you get in?" she cried. "And where's Ellie? If you've harmed her. . .!"

"Hey, hold your horses!" He put the glass down and reached for his pocket. "To answer your first question, I forgot to hand these back. Your keys – remember? And if you're referring to Griselle, she's quite safe. Trust me."

"Trust you!"

"Oh, do I detect a note of bitterness?" he grinned. She saw he was enjoying this. "Griselle's *my* cat, remember. We're very close Almost one, you might say. So of course she's safe. But what do you care, my sweet. I thought you hated cats?"

"Not true. Just never liked them. Couldn't see the attraction. But Ellie's sort of . . . I don't know . . . sort of grown on me."

"Really? I told you she was rather special. It's that third eye, you know. Gives her an extra sense."

"Cobblers! She's not that special. In fact, if you must know, I've been thinking of getting rid of her."

"What!" cried Luke. He was still grinning. *Damn the man!* "Oh, Griselle, did you hear that? She wants rid of you! And without our permission, too."

"I'd be quite within my rights." Emma was riled by his air of self-satisfaction; she was struggling to control herself. "She arrived without my permission, didn't she? But since you ask, she's been pushing her luck lately. Asserting herself a bit too much."

"Really?" he smiled. "Sounds familiar." *Oh, what I would I give to wipe that grin off his face!* "But changing the subject, I'm starving! What's for tea?"

"Fish and chips," she cried. "Fish and chips from the shop on the corner. And you can collect them on your way out of the estate. . ." Forget control: he was the bloody limit! "....on your way out of here, on your way out of my life!" she continued, raising her voice. "For good. My keys, please. You're leaving right now, Luke."

"Really? Oh, I do love you when your dander's up! But have it your way." He levered himself up from the settee and jangled the keys before dropping them onto the coffee table. "Thank you for the drink, my sweet." He moved towards the door. She followed, slightly puzzled by his acquiescence. He's taking it very lightly, she thought. Not like him at all! He stopped and turned. "Emma, it's been great. Really it has. Like I'd never been away!" He offered his hand. "Au revoir."

"We won't be meeting again, Luke," she said, refusing his hand and showing him the front door. "This is final. Trust me."

"Ah, poor sweet! You don't get it, do you? But, like I say, have it your way." And she saw that he was still smiling as he crossed the road to his car. Like it was all part of some game. She stood at the door until he was out of sight.

"Ah, well – that's that. Alone again – thank God! Now for that drink." She made her way back to the sitting room and crossed to her little drinks corner. The gin in last, I think? Yes, I need to taste it. Need a good, strong shot – to wash the taste of him out of my mouth!" She turned to flop onto the sofa – and nearly sat on Ellie!

"Where have you sprung from?" she cried, scooping up the bundle of fur. And she nuzzled and kissed Griselle – something she had never done before – so delighted was she to see her. "Been hiding, have you? Hiding from that nasty old Luke? Don't blame you." But her joy couldn't hide her puzzlement. "The old devil must have been having me on, all along, mustn't he? I might have known – and you, you little mischief, might have warned me, might have shown yourself." She suddenly put the cat down. "But mind this," she said, in mock tones, wagging a warning finger, "if you want to stay, there are going to be some changes around here. Yes, you heard, little Miss Bossy Boots – changes. Drastic changes."

Griselle seemed unimpressed. She had as usual draped herself languidly along the carpet at Emma's feet and was now looking aloofly at her with big, unblinking, amber eyes – for all the world as if she were about to utter, in rather bored tones, "Really?"

GREY'S ELEGY

Russell Grey's wife died one day in late August. He kept her body in the house for three weeks and two days.

It would have been even longer, except he left the door open when he went outside to his little greenhouse in the back garden to pick some tomatoes for her lunch, and the Electric Man called.

He got quite a shock, the Electric Man, as he made his customary way through the sitting room to the little porch where the meters were housed. The weather had been very warm – an Indian summer, folk said – and Rosemary Grey was propped up on the settee smothered in furs and a large double duvet. The central heating was full on, and a large coal fire was burning in the grate. Flies swarmed around the dead woman's head and around the remains of several plates of food left out on the low coffee table. Scores of them made a beeline for the sweat on the Electric Man's face and hands as he dialed 999 on his mobile phone.

There was quite a scene when the police and the medics arrived. Russell's mind had been knocked out of kilter. He couldn't understand why they wanted to take his wife away. "Thirty-seven years!" he kept repeating. "Together thirty-seven years. Please don't take her. She was just cold, poor dear. So cold." He shuddered, as if to emphasize the point. "That's why I added the duvet." He stared vacantly into space. "Just cold, that's all. Off her food, though. Wouldn't touch a thing. Cooked all her favourites, I did – but no! Such a shame. She hates waste. We both do. Brought up during the war, you see." He reached forward and clutched the doctor's arm. "But she'll rally round, you'll see. Just needs more time."

No one was listening. Rosemary was taken away. Then Russell was taken away. They were not taken away together. That was when Russell really lost it – when he was separated from Rosemary. He fought like a cornered animal. One of his flailing arms detonated a police constable's nose. There was blood everywhere.

It was in all the papers, of course. On national television, even. The tiny village community was shocked – but not, on reflection, entirely surprised. The Greys were a devoted couple. They were never seen apart. They had always done everything together. Russell was never seen in the village again.

The Psychiatric Wing of the local hospital was called *The Grove*, perhaps because it backed onto a huddle of mature trees that had once been part of a wide expanse of mixed woodland belonging to the adjoining Lovett Estate. Occasionally, a patient would be seen walking among the trees in the grove. Not one of the paranoiacs, of course. Leaves whispering in the wind, as they sometimes did, could be very threatening to certain patients. But Russell, seeking solace, was soon a regular out there. The trees were his friends, he said. More dependable than people. People betrayed you. They took your loved ones from you. And they told lies. (Had they not told him that his wife was dead?) And you could talk to trees. They didn't argue with you. They didn't try to persuade you to think the way they were thinking. They were neutral; they didn't judge. They listened patiently. They didn't mind you shouting at them, as he sometimes did – as you do from time to time, even with friends.

If not exactly popular – by nature, and by his condition, he kept himself to himself – Russell was a well-liked member of *The Grove* community. Mainly by the staff, it was true – but also by those of his fellow-patients who were able to form relationships. It was hardly surprising. He was polite, mild-mannered and even-tempered. There had been no repercussion of the violence he had demonstrated on the

47

day he was forcibly taken away from his home. Delusional patients could present as quite normal individuals much of the time. As long as their delusions weren't challenged, they could rub along quite smoothly with those around them. In Russell's case, it helped (certainly, with the staff) that he was well-spoken and that his manners were refined. He had quickly acquired the reputation of being something of a gent. Somewhat predictably perhaps, he was soon known to staff and patients alike as *The Earl*.

He continued to protest that Rosemary was still alive, of course. But for the time being, this belief was allowed to go uncontested. To look at him, calmly going about his business, observing the routines of the place, you would never guess that he had a serious psychological problem – so much so that visitors and new patients usually mistook him for a member of staff. The closest he came to exhibiting behaviour that in any way might be regarded as *bizarre* – the word appeared to have some significance in the psychiatric community – occurred several weeks after his admission. By then, Autumn was well under way, and Russell was observed walking among the trees, picking up leaves and bagging them, complaining as he laboured: "They're so untidy! Love them all, of course. Love them to bits, every one of them. But I'm sick of picking up after them. Days getting shorter, too. And colder. Fine time to be taking your clothes off!"

The bags of leaves – at one point there were close on a dozen – began to clutter his room. The cleaners complained that there were so many littering the floor, some of them spilling their contents, that they couldn't do their job properly. The matter became so serious that the senior psychiatrist became involved. Russell was interviewed. Sensitively, of course. Well, he liked the colours, he said. And their different shapes. He liked the smell of them, too, and the crackly sound they made when you disturbed them. Could he keep just *some* of the bags, he pleaded. A long discussion ensued. Eventually, an offer was negotiated. One large bag of leaves – and no more. The senior

48

psychiatrist, Dr Armstrong, was impressed with Russell's willingness to compromise. He recorded as much in his notes.

Autumn deepened. The trees in the grove had shed almost all of their gaudy, tattered clothing. Their forlorn trunks and limbs and branching fingers could be seen black and wet against the setting sun. It disturbed Russell to see them in this condition. Their arms seemed to be thrown up to the sky, as if pleading for some respite from the cold. But their entreaties went unheeded. Temperatures began to fall, and in an increasingly chilly wind the naked branches would sometimes shiver visibly. Some of the older trees would creak and groan, complaining among themselves about the cold getting into their joints. Russell shivered and suffered with them – for he refused to walk warmly-clad among his friends. They, poor things, had little or nothing to wear. How could he flaunt his advantage? The very thought was obscene.

One day in early December, Russell went missing for a few hours. He did not appear for lunch: that was when a search was instigated. The first place they looked was the grove, of course; but there was no sign of him in there. No sign of him anywhere, in fact. The search was extended to the main building, and finally to the grounds of the hospital. Then suddenly – at a point when the police were about to be involved – the hunt was called off. Russell had been found in his beloved grove after all. No one had thought to check it out again.

It was Adrian, one of the gardeners, who found him. Russell was perched three rungs from the top of a long metal ladder, which was propped up against the bough of an old oak tree. A large bag hung from a length of string slung around his waist. Every couple of minutes or so, he dipped a hand into this bag before reaching up into the branches of the tree. By now it was getting on for three o'clock, with the light beginning to fade. Adrian couldn't make out what Russell was

49

doing. But whatever it was, it demanded all his attention. Rapt in his work, he seemed totally unaware that he was being observed.

"Ah, there you are!" Adrian had called up, grasping the foot of the ladder with two strong hands, vibrating it slightly. "Glad I've found you. High and low, we've been searching. You old rogue! Led us a right dance, you have." Russell had ignored him. Absorbed in his task, he had carried on. Adrian caught a movement in one of the branches. "Best come down, eh? Dark soon. Could get tricky then. What're you doing up there, any road?"

"What does it look like?"

"I dunno. Can't see in this light. What's in the bag?"

"Leaves, of course." Russell had lowered his hands, and had turned his body to look down. "One of the gardeners, aren't you – yes? Well, you of all people should know about my friends in here. Winter's coming on. You must have noticed? Poor things, they're going to freeze unless we get some clothes back on them. Believe me, I know. Take my word, I know about these things. So that's what I'm – oh, bugger! Now look what's happened. I've got glue on my hands!"

"Not sure I've quite got your drift, my friend," Adrian had called up. "But whatever you're doing, best get down now, eh? You can't work in the dark."

"Don't want to come down," Russell had cried. "Job unfinished." His voice was cracking. Was he crying, Adrian had wondered? "But anyway – I can't come down. Not now. I seem to be stuck to the ladder!"

Someone had to come from the hospital. He came with a ladder, a patient manner and a special solvent. He left unable to conceal a smile. Russell was left to face a new round of friendly chats with Dr Armstrong. Dr Armstrong also wore a smile. Such a nice man, Russell thought. Everyone was very kind and friendly. But only Dr Armstrong seemed to understand why the sticking-back-on of the leaves had been so important to him.

Winter set in. Snow. Rain. Cloud. Wind. Occasional sunshine – but usually accompanied by numbing cold. The sort of weather that didn't encourage walks among the trees. Not that Russell was able to go out for several weeks. He went down with pneumonia, and his convalescence was slow. He found it difficult to regain his former vigour. More worryingly, he seemed to have lost all interest in life. He fretted about the fate of his beloved trees. He shut himself away whenever possible. He seemed to hibernate within himself. He began to exhibit signs of depression. Dr Armstrong and his team were worried.

Caroline, Russell's daughter, was summoned from New Zealand. She left behind her rosy-cheeked apple-grower, Reuben, and her two teenage girls. But not for long, she hoped. God willing, this business with her Dad would soon be settled one way or another. These things took time, she realized. People grieved in different ways. But for heaven's sake, it had been months now! *Maybe the last throw of the dice,* the doctor had said. So, yes – she was willing to give it another go. "But don't hold your breath," she had warned. They had never been close, she and her Dad. His cozy intimacy with her mother had always left her feeling excluded.

She was given a room in the Wing. To be near her father. So they could talk. There was a lot of talking – on her part, anyway. She observed a change in him. A change for the better, perhaps? He seemed less prickly, much more resigned.

With Dr Armstrong's blessing, she decided to take him to the place where her mother's ashes were scattered. The site was a limestone outcrop on the southern slopes of Wild Boar Hill, a peaceful spot overlooking a ribbon of water that wound its ways through the narrow valley below. It was less than a mile from the road, and no more than a hundred yards or so to the east of the main footpath. Yet it felt remote. She hired a taxi for the twelve-mile round trip. It waited for them in the small lay-by tucked into the foot of the hill.

"Why have we come here?" Russell asked.

"I told you, remember?" Caroline took a cushion from her bag for him to sit on. "To be near Mum."

"No," Russell said. His voice was low, but firm. "Your mother's in the hospital. Be out soon. I told you – remember? So why are we here?"

"Okay, Dad, have it your way." Caroline was counting to ten. "Let's say we're here so that I can be close to Mum."

"Sorry. . .?"

"She loved this spot, Dad. Don't you remember?"

"No, I don't. Never been here before."

"Yes, you have. Dozens of times. Honestly, Dad – your favourite view!" She turned to look at him and attempted a smile. Her shock tactics were not working. She looked at the view again. "Well, anyway – I feel close. Let's leave it at that, shall we?" Hearing the crack in her voice, she paused. "She's only three feet away. So, yes – I feel close." She turned her head again. "Bit of a shock for me as well, you know – living on the other side of the world."

Russell didn't respond. He stared at the ground ahead of them. For several quiet, painful minutes, he simply sat, still as the rock beneath him, and stared at the ribs of limestone poking through the short, sheep-nibbled grass.

"God, it's cold here!" he said suddenly, and he shuddered. "And the ground – so bare! What a dreadful place to be! I want to go, please. I want to leave. Please will you take me away?"

A fortnight after Caroline went back to North Island, New Zealand, Russell went missing again. This time, the police were involved. This time, Dr Armstrong and his team were seriously concerned. The search went on for thirty-six hours, and there was still no sign of him.

Eventually – in retrospect, perhaps it should have been done sooner? – Caroline was contacted again. She told them about the visit to Wild Boar Hill. She gave them the name of the taxi firm she had used – and yes, a man fitting Russell's description had hired a cab the previous day. It was a one-way fare.

The search party arrived at the outcrop towards late afternoon on the second day. In front of the memorial seat they found a pile of men's clothing, neatly folded, covering the ground like a blanket. Socks, rolled neatly into a pair of shoes, were found alongside. A large piece of limestone had been placed on top of the clothing, presumably to stop it blowing away in what was known locally as a "thin" wind. There was no sign of Russell.

He was found twenty minutes later in a right-angled corner between two dry stone walls, about a quarter of a mile up the slope. It was a place obviously favoured by sheep seeking refuge from the elements. There was a strong smell of droppings, and scraps of wool caught in the crevices between the stones were being spun in small spirals of air that had breached the sheltering wall.

Russell was stark naked and curled up like a foetus. His neat, close-together knees were drawn up to his chest, and his arms were thrown across his body, as if for warmth. He was, however, as cold as the stone around him. And his lifeless body was so stiff that his knee-joints had later to be broken before he could be laid out.

THE CROSSING

He was relieved to be off the train. *So many people! They couldn't all be making the crossing, surely? No, of course they couldn't.* In fact, as he trudged out of the station towards the flower-bordered boulevard, the human stream had already begun to fan out, dispersing passengers in a dozen different directions. *Silly man!* There were a hundred and one other reasons for people to be out and about today. But it was easy to forget that – especially when your mind, your whole being, was focused on one thing, as his had been for weeks now. Ever since he had contacted the Agency to finalize the booking, he had been unable to think of anything else.

On the broad pavement of the boulevard leading to the port, he checked his watch and slowed down. He had plenty of time. Time to appreciate the Spring flowers, to smell the orange blossom, to enjoy the sun on his back and the gentle breeze on his face; time indeed, now that he was no longer being jostled, to relax his mind and his body, the way he had been instructed in the manual. He had always hated crowds: the noise, the press, the heat, the smell, the raw power and potential menace. It was a relief now to have a little space around him. Yet the crowds back there, on the train and in the station, had been a timely, if slightly uneasy, reminder that what he was doing was for the best. It hadn't been a simple decision. This was life as he knew it, in the land of his birth. He didn't want to leave. But one had to think of the future.

"Good afternoon, sir," greeted the official behind the desk at Reception. He was a slightly built, pasty-faced young man who looked as if he were in need of a break in the *Sunshine Isles* himself. "Good journey?"

"Not really. Glad it's almost over. The trains were very crowded."

"Always are, sir. Ever since petrol rationing. And road charges, of course. But at least it's safer crossing the street these days." He paused, and for the first time he appeared to take note of his client. "Anyway, you're here now, sir. You came along Sunset Boulevard, I take it? Yes, most people do. It's the obvious route – and quite the best way, I always think, to complete this part of your journey. Fairly quiet this time of day, I assume?"

"Yes. Quite a relief. Those crowds made me realize suddenly how important. . ."

"Of course, sir," interrupted the official. "I understand. You don't need to explain. Now, can I trouble you for your name and booking number, please?"

"Pendleton's my name. Christopher Pendleton. And my. . ." he hesitated for a moment, before taking a piece of paper from his breast pocket and checking it, "my number is VR389426. Sorry about that. I had hoped to memorize it, but they're such long numbers."

"No problem, sir," said the young man. "I'd already got you on my screen." He spoke with the practised ease of someone who had followed the same routine, day in, day out, for longer than he cared to remember. "And your mother's maiden name, sir? If you wouldn't mind? For security reasons, you understand?"

"Of course. Moffat – Moffat with a double 'f' and one 't'.

"Thank you, sir, that's wonderful. Now. . . " he intoned, "you left your main luggage at the station – yes? Good: don't worry, the Agency will take care of all that. And your hand luggage, sir? Packed by you, and you alone – yes? Excellent, sir. Can't be too careful, can we?" His smile seemed to writhe Heap-like across his face. "Now, sir," he continued, pecking at a pad with a long, bony finger, "in a moment I will hand you over to Sharon who will escort you to the hospitality room in the First Class departure lounge. There you can help yourself to drinks and freshen up before being conducted to your berth." He

55

hesitated slightly before proceeding. "But first, on the subject of berths, may I enquire if you are still willing to share? And if so, would you prefer to share with a male or a female?"

"Good lord, I didn't realize I had a choice! Well, it might depend, of course. . .? But why not? Start of an adventure, and all that – so yes, let's take a chance. Bit of female company – not had much of that since. . ." He paused, his eyes becoming misty. "Yes, might as well make the crossing as pleasurable as possible, eh? I say, this is quite a service!"

"Well, sir, we do try to please." *Had his lips moved towards a smile? Or was it another writhe?* "It has always been Agency policy," he continued in a mechanical voice, "to give special consideration to our VR-category passengers. As we see it, sir, your status deserves no less. So, a berth shared with a lady – yes?"

"Yes, I think so. Willing to take a chance, anyway."

"Splendid, sir. You won't be disappointed, I can promise you. All Agency pairings are determined strictly scientifically, using the very latest sociometric and psychometric techniques. They come with a guarantee. In fourteen months, since we started handling retirement crossings, we have never had a single complaint." He paused before proceeding with his well-rehearsed script. "Well, I think that is all, sir. Except to say that I am glad to have played my humble part in processing your booking – and, of course, to wish you *bon voyage* on behalf of the Agency. The forecast, by the way, is for a very smooth crossing. So enjoy, sir. And perhaps you will now kindly follow Sharon?"

Sharon had short blonde hair, styled into a close-fitting helmet. She wore powder-blue trousers, with matching high-necked tunic, and white, soft-leather sneakers. Her oval face wore a fixed smile that looked as if it had been painted on with her make-up. Christopher tried to estimate her age, but gave up. She could have been anywhere between twenty-five and fifty-five: he really had no idea. Nor could he be certain, despite her name, that she was indeed a woman, for there were no curves to her slender form. There were no vocal clues to go on, either: she led the way in silence.

In the hospitality room he poured himself a robust gin-and-tonic and took it with him into the shower. After drying, he helped himself to another drink of similar strength which he sipped as he dressed. This second shot made him feel warm and carefree, but it also made his head swim a little. If he had overdone it slightly – if he had poured the gin *with a palsied hand*, as his dear wife used to joke – well, so what. He was, after all, about to embark on a momentous journey. What did it matter? What did anything matter? At his age, and at this stage of his life, one took one's little pleasures at every opportunity.

The androgynous Sharon was waiting for him when he returned to the main body of the departure lounge. She led him towards a passenger conveyance that moved them silently through a long, narrow passageway whose oval walls were lined with fine art prints. After two or three minutes, she signalled him to step off the moving platform and to follow her along a short corridor. She stopped outside a white door where, with the touch of a finger, she activated a security pad. The door to his berth opened silently inwards.

He turned to his escort, intending to thank her; but, totally fazed by her inscrutable silence, he found himself incapable of making a sound. It was unnerving: her body position, the angle of her head, the line of her smile – everything about her – was just as it was when he first saw her. Nothing had changed. Except. . .? Yes, as she was about to turn away, did he detect a slight hesitation? Almost as if she wanted to say something? He felt a sudden pang of compassion for her. Not much of a job, was it? Ferrying people you would never see again from one area of a terminus to another? He produced a twenty-pound coin from his pocket and pressed the silver piece into her palm. With a slight inclination of her head, nothing more, she slipped the coin discreetly into the breast pocket of her tunic and departed.

Christopher's companion for the crossing was a woman named Hermione Darwin. They got on splendidly from the start; in their case, the Agency had got the *matching* process exactly right. Like himself, Hermione had opted for the voluntary package, as opposed to waiting, as most people did, for compulsory orders – so they had something in common from the start.

"Yes, I couldn't see the point of going on till I was forced out at seventy," she said, in her down-to-earth fashion. "I mean, don't get me wrong, I'm quite happy here – and I'm still sound of wind and limb, as you see – but a few more months are neither here nor there, are they? Might as well go early and qualify for the special concessions. Face up to it, old girl, I said. Country's too small: population's too big. Simple mathematics. Accept the inevitable. Jump before you're pushed!"

"Yes, I had to give it a lot of thought," said Christopher. "It's a big step, after all. But my reasoning went roughly along the same lines. Anyway, decision's made now. So, what say we break into that champagne?"

Hermione was a heavy-featured woman, unfashionably dressed, with a large, intimidating frontage. Physically she was rather unappealing: not his type at all. But she had twinkling eyes, a keen intelligence and a fund of interesting stories. Born in Australia, she had come to England to do archaeology at Cambridge, and had then travelled the world on 'digs' – one of which, near Ephesus, had brought her brief fame on television. He remembered now: *Digger Darwin*, they used to call her. More recently, and with the same energy, she had taken up gardening, specializing in medicinal plants, including cannabis – which, she told him unashamedly, she had been taking with her food for years.

"Great for my arthritis – not to mention my dreams! And," she twinkled, "I happen to have brought some with me. Like to try a joint?

58

Or would you rather have one of my little *space cakes*?" She giggled. "I gave one to that creep on the desk, to have with his afternoon cuppa. So there might well be the odd mismatch this evening, I reckon. Serve the little bastard right!" She paused, seeing Christopher's face. "Yeah, I know: not so funny for the couples concerned, maybe. But it'll make life interesting for 'em – and I'm all for that, eh?"

Christopher was about to respond when the doorbell rang. It was the waiter – all done up in bow tie and tails: Hermione couldn't conceal her mirth – delivering the evening meal on a beautifully decked trolley, resplendent with covered silver salvers, silver candelabrum and a silver vase containing a single red rose, at the sight of which Hermione began to chuckle.

"Voila," said the waiter, removing the lids with the flourish of a magician. "As ordered, a 25:36:26 for madame, and a 25:58:26 for monsieur. Bon appetit."

The fresh crab starter was delicious, they agreed; and they found it interesting that, as with the dessert, they had chosen the same dish. However, at times Hermione could hardly eat for laughing.

"A 25:36:26," she kept repeating. "I wish! Though there was a time. . ."

Once the meal was over, she sat back and chuckled again. "Can't get over it!" she said. "The flunkey, the red rose, all that ceremonial crap – and for what: food by numbers, Chinese take-away style!"

"Yes, but the best take-away I've ever had," said Christopher. "I thought it was excellent."

It was a different man who came to take away the trolley, but like his colleague he was impeccably dressed and professionally polite.

"I am delighted to hear that you enjoyed your meal," he said, seemingly unaware of Hermione's lingering mirth. "Now, please help yourselves to drinks from the cabinet. In five minutes time there will be a visual presentation on the big, white wall in your lounging area. I recommend it; it will tell you all you need to know about your

59

destination. So, take to the recliners, lie back and enjoy. You're probably not aware of it – today's conditions in the Orchnae Channel are uncommonly calm – but the crossing is now under way. The captain reports from the bridge that the sun has just dropped down below the horizon, so be warned: it will turn a little chilly shortly. But do not worry: your berth is centrally heated, with the thermostat set to accord with outside temperatures. The heating will probably click on in the next few minutes. Please ring if you require further assistance. Otherwise, sit back, enjoy a drink, enjoy one another's company, enjoy the presentation; and if you happen to fall asleep – well, not to worry: we guarantee to wake you up in time to see the Retirement Isles come into view. Good night. If not before, I will see you on the other side."

"Can't really fault them, can you?" said Christopher, after the door had closed silently behind the waiter. "I know it's a bit over the top, some of it, but you have to hand it to them: it's all highly professional, if. . . "

"If without soul, you mean?" said Hermione. "All a load of bollocks, if you ask me. Can't take it seriously myself." She smiled across at him. "But at least the company's good."

"Relieved to hear it, Digger Darwin," he laughed. "Now, what say we have a double brandy – and maybe one of your space cakes – and go through to watch the movie?"

"You're on," laughed Hermione. "You pour the brandies, I'll get the cookies."

The presentation, which began seconds after they took to their recliners, was slickly produced.

"Welcome to *Las Islas de la Jubilacion*," it began. "The Retirement Isles, as they are popularly called, are five jewels set in the long, sparkling necklace of islands called on the map, the Acherusian Archipelago, but more usually referred to as *Las Islas del Sol* – The Sunshine Islands – because of their tropical location. Formerly a

Spanish possession, they became part of the old British Empire towards the end of the nineteenth century. Your accommodation – consisting, as you see, of spacious bungalows built beneath swaying palms – is located on the cool coastal fringes. It will be noted that each bungalow is comfortably furnished, and fully equipped to the highest modern standards, and – how about this, folks! – each unit of four shares this attractive leisure pool. All provisions are brought to your door in these quaint electric floats – so no noise, no smell! – and full medical care is available 24/7. You need never leave the complex – your home, indeed – unless you wish to; but if you want to be adventurous, the islands offer a varied topography and plenty of places of interest. So, you lucky people, imagine yourselves there already – reclining by the pool or on the beach, a sun-downer in your hand, a gentle breeze on your cheek, listening to the sound of the sea breaking gently on the shore, with not a care in the world."

At this point Christopher turned to Hermione, fully expecting to receive an explosive retort along the lines of *what bland, promotional pap to be feeding intelligent people who still had enough teeth to chew on more demanding fare!* But she was fast asleep.

"Night, night, Digger," he whispered. "Sweet cannabis dreams!"

He settled back in his recliner and returned his eyes to the screen, in time to see yet another strand of silver sand lapped by a pacific, gently susurrating sea. The sea's peaceful sibilance was all around him now. It seemed to come through the very walls themselves, reminding him oddly of the gas-fire he and Liz used to have in the early days of their marriage.

"Ah, well, Hermione," he said quietly, closing his eyes. He had suddenly become very drowsy. "You're right – time to go. Time to give way to sleep. See you in the morning, old girl. See you on the other side."

A DARKER SHADE OF NIGHT

She picked the berries – round, black, like small cherries – in the dead of night.

It was a black-eyed, belladonna sort of night, with a darkness she could touch, a darkness that clung to her clothing as she glided between the high hedges, cobwebs trailing from her face.

She knew where to stop; knew the exact spot; knew where to start plucking with deft fingers the smooth, black shapes from the shapeless darkness.

In her kitchen the next morning, as she worked the sliced berries into a cake mixture with her bony fingers, she found herself reading aloud from a piece of card propped up against a flour bag. Her voice was shrill with excitement.

Symptoms begin with dryness of the mouth and tongue, and some difficulty in swallowing. A rash develops on the upper body; a headache and giddiness give way to hallucinations, then to delirium. Later, paralysis, sleep, coma. Death is due to respiration failure. Pupils are so dilated that eyes appear black.

She paused, laughing to herself, before reading on:

The witches of old prepared ointments from belladonna, which they then massaged into their vaginas to bring on wild hallucinations, to create a sensation of flying.

The cake went into the oven. She cackled her satisfaction.

"There, Henry," she cooed that afternoon. "A treat for your tea. Your favourite: a nice cherry cake."

"No thank you, dear." Henry's voice was cold, mechanical. "I've gone off cherry cake. *Your* cherry cake, anyway. And your wholesome mushroom soup. Simply lost my appetite for them. Can't think why."

He knew! The old bugger knew.

No – of course he didn't. Even he couldn't access the dark recesses of her mind.

She now fell to musing. . .

Fly Agaric: Amanita muscaria.

Deadly Nightshade: Atropa belladonna.

Strychnine: Strychnos nux vomica. . .

She chanted the names in a sing-song voice, intoning like a priestess. Oh, such a shame! Like poetry, they were, those names. So musical. Music you could die to, surely?

Oh, damn the man! He was spoiling things, as usual. Thoughts of toxic fungi and deadly nightshade would now have to be abandoned – along with herbicides, pesticides, bullet, blade, bludgeon, suffocation, electrocution. The list was far from exhaustive, but it had soon exhausted her. She had given up counting after nine.

It was shortly after he came out of hospital that she had finally decided Henry had to go.

They hadn't kept him in for long. They didn't these days. More was the pity. But those eight blissful days were the happiest of her married life.

Oh, the freedom! No cooking: she ate out, most of the time. No catatonic evenings in front of the television: she went to the theatre twice. No dreading the bedtimes: with no one lumpy and snoring and sweating in her bed, the nights became her favourite time. No abstinence: she got through three bottles of gin while he was away. She was even on the verge of getting off with a chap in the bar of the

Civic Theatre – until, that is, she reminded herself that it might be men she was seeking freedom from.

It was like being single again. No one arguing with her decisions, or carping, or complaining. No one finding fault. The silence was eloquent, music to her ears.

The contrast was what finally made up her mind for her. For if Henry had been difficult before he went into hospital, he was at once impossible when he came out.

The hospital had saved his life, he declared. It had not only opened his abdomen, it had opened his eyes. Delicious food, comfortable beds, impeccable standards of hygiene – and above all, devoted care and attention. In fact, so wonderful were the nursing staff that he had invited one of them to come and have a meal with them a fortnight after his discharge.

Staff-nurse Jenkins – "Amie, with an 'ie'," she had introduced herself – was big and blowzy, loud and confident. Maureen didn't take to her one bit. Henry, though, was clearly quite smitten. Each time Maureen returned to the room from the kitchen, there they were, on the settee, *tete a tete*, chatting away about the hospital. It was the same during the meal: Henry and Amie, chatting in a warm bubble of intimacy from which she was totally excluded.

There was a row about it afterwards.

That had been the turning point. That was when the plotting had started. Henry had to go!

But how? By what means? Poison was a mad-cap idea. Too detectable. And the other methods were either too messy or too contrived. She was getting desperate. There had to be another way, a cleverer way. A way that would avoid detection. She spent night after night, lying in the darkness, racking her brains for the answer. The perfect crime; was there such a thing?

One day, right out of the blue, he suggested a weekend away. In Robin Hood's Bay, of all places, where they had honeymooned, where their ill-fated marriage had begun. They would stay at the same hotel, he announced, and revisit their favourite haunts.

"Ah," he enthused, "those beautiful, quiet beaches, those towering, majestic cliffs. It'll do us both good."

She was amazed – so astounded that she gave herself one of her headaches trying to work out what his little game might be. Not seeking any kind of reconciliation, she hoped. Because if he was, he could forget it.

She remained puzzled, but she decided to go along with the idea. More out of curiosity than anything. On one or two occasions recently, she had come upon him unexpectedly and had found him smiling. Not his usual weasel smile. More your enigmatic, Mona Liza, *I-know-something-you-don't-know* sort of smile. What was he playing at? She had no idea, but she was determined to be civil, at least.

For his part, Henry was civility itself. He had booked two *single* rooms – thank goodness! – and there were no snide comments, no criticisms, no put-downs. It was amazing. Not like Henry at all.

On the second night she announced her intention to take a short stroll along the cliffs before dinner.

"Yes, you always loved that walk." Henry looked pleased. "Think I'll take a turn with you. Do you mind?"

He had asked so politely that she felt she could hardly refuse. When she suggested taking the car as close as they could to the path in order to spend as much time as possible on the cliff-top, Henry had meekly agreed. She couldn't get over how reasonable he was being.

They walked in silence much of the time. He seemed to be in a reflective mood, and she was pleased to be left to her own thoughts. She wasn't sure she trusted this new, accommodating Henry. He normally disliked walking, and his recent surgery would have given him every excuse to decline. But he stayed the course, without complaint.

In fact, at the end, he seemed reluctant to return to the car. He stood on the cliff-top, rock-still, for ages, saying nothing, just staring out to sea. She enjoyed the view with him for a few minutes. It was magnificent. The setting sun was suffusing the water with a liquid gold, creating a Turneresque canvas which kept changing in pattern, tone and texture with the movement of the sea.

Suddenly she shivered violently.

"What's the matter, dear?" he said, coming out of his reverie. "Someone walk over your grave?"

"No, just getting cold, that's all," she replied. "We ought to be getting back."

"Nonsense!" he cried. "Don't spoil the moment, dear. We've plenty of time. They don't stop serving till nine."

"As you wish," she said, "but I'll have to go for a cardigan."

When she returned twenty minutes later he was still standing where she had left him, staring out to sea, motionless. His back looked broad and dark and solid in what was now a failing light.

"Careful!" she almost cried out, dredging the word up from a time all those years ago when she might have worried for his safety.

But another thought quickly intruded.

Oh, the irony! All those weeks of plotting – and here, suddenly, by chance! It was a perfect opportunity. All too easy, surely?

"No, go for it! *Carpe diem*. Careful, though. Don't rush it. Stealth is called for. Stealth and control. Take your time. Move quietly. On velvet paw. That's it – last few yards. Nearly there. Hold your nerve. Rough ground, remember. Heather hiding rock. And fading light. Watch your feet. Good – that's it. Control your approach. Control your breathing. Yes, perfect. Almost there. One final step. One firm push. Exit Henry!"

She put all her force into the lunge; but just as her hands went forward she noticed, too late, that Henry's head – that faintly ridiculous head of his, far too small for his body, the beaky nose far too large for its face – was half-turned towards her. He couldn't have heard her approach, surely? No, it was almost as if he had anticipated it? *Oh, my God!* But the realization came too late. Henry suddenly, very neatly, sidestepped to his left, leaving her off-balance, pushing against the evening air.

For a long, terrifying second there was a desperate flailing of arms as she fought to regain her balance. Her frightened eyes, popping out from her anguished face, flashed sideways at Henry, pleading for assistance. Her mouth flew open, releasing a shriek of terror. It was answered only by the cry of a passing black-headed gull.

Henry smiled.

"Oh, are you off now, dear?" he enquired, as she commenced her fall.

His voice was drowned in a rush of air as she plummeted down at breath-taking speed to the rack of rock and sea, to the brief smack of splintering pain, waiting in the black, final black, night below.

"I see. Going without a word, are we? How rude!"

His smile grew broader.

"Never mind. Night, night, dear."

THE BIRD HOUSE

The Pet Shop man kept the birdseed in small sacks on the floor in front of his feet; to reach them he had to duck down so low that his head was now at counter level. Charlotte looked across at his mop of frizzy ginger hair and smiled. It was like an untidy nest, she thought. Indeed at that very moment, through the flickering light from a line of tropical fish tanks to her left, several small birds from the cages behind him seemed to fly in and flutter about in it.

"There you are, me duck," he said, banging the sack down on the counter. "That'll be three fifty-five." His nest caught the light again, but the birds had flown. "Things alright, are they? You know – with the Captain and his new cage?"

"Joseph," corrected Charlotte abruptly, and she suddenly went all hot.

"Sorry, me duck, I" m not with you?"

"Joseph," repeated Charlotte. "From the Bible. That's Captain Flint's new name."

"Ah, I see," he said. "The old pirate sent packing. Made to walk the plank." He laughed at his little joke. "Joseph, eh? The bloke with the coat of many colours, yes?" Charlotte nodded. "Very clever. I like that. And the cage?"

"Oh, fine," said Charlotte, avoiding his beady eyes, looking instead at the assortment of simulated dog bones displayed in a box below the fish tanks. "Very big, though. Bigger than I expected. Fills the room, almost."

"Well, I did show you the dimensions." His tone was defensive. "Remember?"

"Yes, of course," said Charlotte. "It's my own fault, I know that."

"Anyway – enjoying his new quarters is he, the Captain? Sorry, Joseph! You know – the extra space?"

"I think so." Charlotte hesitated. "Not at first, though. And it was quite a performance, transferring him. He escaped and flew about the room. Went absolutely wild. Even bit me!"

"Well, I did warn you," said the storekeeper. "Not hand-reared, you see."

"Yes, he is a bit unruly. But I'm hoping he might change with all the extra attention I can give him, now that. . . "

"Yes, I was sorry to hear about your dad. Can't be easy for you." He paused. "Any road, I wish you all the best with Joseph. Don't expect too much, though. Not with macaws. Notorious for villainy, is macaws."

"Don't you worry, I won't," laughed Charlotte. "You can – "

She broke off suddenly.

"Oh, they're lovely! Quite lovely."

He looked puzzled.

"Those little things in your. . . " She checked herself. The light was playing tricks again. "In that cage behind you. What are they?"

He turned his head. "Ah, they're finches, me duck. Zebra finches. Yes, they're pretty, all right."

"And what about those?" asked Charlotte, pointing a finger over a pile of cat baskets. "Those in that cage over there, the two together? Yes, those two? What are they called?"

"They're your lovebirds," he smiled. "Only sold in pairs, they are." He inclined his head and winked. Somewhat lewdly, she thought. "Yes, always canoodling, they are. Real lovebirds."

"Oh, what beautiful little things!" cooed Charlotte, putting an errant strand of her mousy hair back in place. "So small – and so agreeable." She took out her purse. "But I must dash. Got someone coming this afternoon."

"Here we are," Charlotte announced, entering her parlour with a large tray, which she set down on the coffee table. "Now, milk and no sugar – that right?" She handed Marion the cup and saucer. "Can I offer you a tart? Shop-bought, I'm afraid – but they're fresh. Fresh this morning. Or a biscuit? Please help yourself."

"I'd be careful there," warned Nancy, pointing a bony finger at the chair as Charlotte turned to sit. "There's something on the seat. Be a shame to soil your nice clean dress."

"Oh, I am sorry," said Charlotte, flushing up as she nipped the dried bird dropping with a tissue. She shot a black look in Joseph's direction as she took up her perch on the edge of the chair. "Anyway, what do you think?"

"Well, it's different, that's for sure." Nancy laughed. "So big – and so close. Almost as if we're the ones inside the cage – with our friend over there looking in, sizing us up."

Charlotte watched Nancy's sharp-edged Adam's-apple bob about in her scrawny neck. She doesn't like it, she thought, at once feeling panicky.

"Trouble is," Nancy went on, "I remember this room in the old days when your mother and father were alive. So cosy, then. Always a cheerful fire in the grate. Cumfy three-piece suite. Knick-knacks in the china cabinet. Such a lovely room, I always thought." She paused, lifting her teacup. "What's happened to it all, by the way? The furniture?"

"In the passage, most of it," explained Charlotte. "The rest is upstairs, in dad's old. . . in the spare room." She took in a deep breath. "You don't like it, do you? A bigger cage, you said. But you don't like it. I can tell."

There was an awkward silence, broken only by the continuous chuntering and muttering coming from Joseph's discourteous back as he continuously shifted his weight from one foot to the other.

"Well, he's certainly got plenty of space now," Nancy said eventually. "Never seen one so big. Except in the Arboretum."

"Not too keen on him either, are you?" Charlotte could hardly believe her boldness. "I sense that, too."

"Oh, he's handsome enough, I'll grant him that," said Nancy, looking across at Joseph's fine plumage. "In a flashy, gaudy sort of fashion. If you like that sort of thing." She paused, adjusting her gold-rimmed spectacles on her sharp little nose, as if the better to bring him into focus. "Not very friendly, though," she went on, lifting her cup to her thin lips. She took a sip. "In fact, a bit rude really, the way he turns his back on you like that. And does he actually say anything? Apart from all that muttering, I mean. Does he ever talk — you know, say things you can understand?"

"Oh goodness me, yes," laughed Charlotte. "Quite a lot, when I'm alone with him. And naughty things, sometimes. Things to make you blush."

"You don't mean he swears?" Nancy's tone was acidly disapproving.

"Yes, I'm afraid he does sometimes," admitted Charlotte, risking another nervous little laugh. Then she saw the look of disgust on Nancy's face and immediately regretted her levity.

"Oh, I wouldn't stand for that," Nancy said, holding her second lemon curd tart in suspension inches below her mouth.

Almost as if he'd heard and understood, Joseph turned up the volume on his ill-mannered chuntering. Then, lifting one foot higher than usual as he shifted his weight, he chose the precise moment that Nancy bit into her tart to squirt one of his big, ploppy messes all too audibly onto the floor of his cage.

"Really!" cried Nancy, choking on a mixture of pastry crumbs and indignation. "How disgusting!"

" Oh, you get used to it. And you can't blame him. Not his fault. It's what birds do."

71

"But can't he be trained, or something?" Nancy queried, picking spluttered crumbs from the skirt of her navy-blue two-piece. "Like you do with a dog?"

Charlotte laughed. "I'm afraid not. And anyway, it's too late for this old reprobate. About seventy years too late."

Joseph had kept quite still for the last couple of minutes; but now, almost as if he wanted to demonstrate how much he resented these criticisms, he suddenly let out a terrifying squawk, flew round the cage two or three times, and then came crashing into the bars at high speed right next to Nancy, his flinty grappling irons striking the wire with a loud clatter. The force of his impact set the cage ringing loudly and sent up a chaotic flurry of dust particles and small feathers which could be seen for seconds afterwards charging about in the up-draught.

Nancy's cup rattled in its saucer, sending her half-drunk tea spilling onto her skirt and dripping down to the carpet. She shot to her feet, handed the china to Charlotte and began dabbing at her skirt with a hanky. Then, coughing suddenly as the disturbed parrot dust caught in her throat, she made for the door.

Charlotte forgave Joseph. It was the Christian thing to do. After all, he was only a bird. Thereafter, however, she found herself devoting less and less time to him — unlike the early days, before the advent of the new cage, when she would sometimes spend an hour or two each day in the parlour, talking to him, trying to develop a relationship, trying to improve his limited vocabulary. Hoping to civilize him a little. But she got very little response. In fact, despite his acquired biblical credentials, it soon emerged that his language could be even more colourful than his gaudy plumage. Disappointingly, his behaviour seemed to get worse rather than better after he was moved to his new quarters.

One morning he committed an unforgivable sin.

72

"Jesus!" he squawked, suddenly. "Jesus Christ!" Then he paused, as if calculating the impact of what was to follow. "Jesus Christ, Jesus Christ, Jesus Christ," he croaked, again and again.

Charlotte was shocked. "Blasphemer!" she cried, shaking his cage so violently that she almost dislodged him from his perch. "Evil blasphemer!"

The real showdown came a day or so later when she entered his cage to give it what her mother used to call "a good bottoming". As usual, she ducked down to crawl through the door-opening on her hands and knees, a manoeuvre which inevitably meant taking her eyes off the bird. She was about to straighten up and turn towards his perch, when suddenly he took off, swooped low and strafed her with his claws.

"Aaah!" she cried, as she felt his cruel nails gouge her scalp.

She put her hands to her head for protection. They felt sticky. He had drawn blood!

"Get off, you brute – get off!" she yelled, flapping her arms frantically, trying to shoo him back to his perch.

But Joseph wouldn't settle. As she crawled backwards out of the cage, he came diving down again. She screamed, got to her feet and made for the parlour door. As she closed it, she saw him flutter out of the cage and fly up to the curtain rail. He was free again.

"That's it," she yelled at the door panels. "No more. I wash my hands of you." She was still reeling from the violence of the attack. "And it's Flint again, okay? You're renamed. Joseph's too good for you." She paused to get her breath back. "Yes, re-named – not re-christened. Christian names are not for heathens like you."

She always meant to go back in. Always meant to return him to his cage, if she could. But she kept putting it off. She was afraid of him now. Also, it had been such a performance the last time. She couldn't face that again. One day, perhaps.

Meanwhile she kept him alive by sliding dishes of food and water through the partially opened door of the parlour, sometimes receiving a painful bite from his hooked beak in return for her charity. Of course, it worried her that she was unable to clean him out. But it couldn't be helped: he had brought it upon himself. He would just have to live in his own filth for a while. Until he learned some manners.

Flint" s violent attack had left her feeling depressed and weepy. But things were about to change. From her next visit to the pet shop she returned home with a pair of lovebirds: the very pair, the storekeeper assured her, that she had admired so much before.

It was an impulsive purchase, but one that brightened her life instantly. For she quickly fell in love with her sweet-natured companions. Indeed, they delighted her so much that a few days later she went back to the shop and bought two more. Then four quickly became eight, and eight became sixteen – and so on, until within a very short time she had scores and scores of small birds in cages all over the house. Just how many, she soon lost count.

They were not all lovebirds, of course. Charlotte quickly diversified, acquiring many other species: canaries, parakeets, lorikeets, finches and cockatiels. She read books about small birds, and she began to take the Caged Birds magazine from her newsagent. Gaining confidence, she even contacted local breeders, and inspired by these enthusiasts she started breeding herself.

"Well, you know, not me, of course," she giggled to one of her friends at church. "My birds, I mean."

She loved all her birds. Loved feeding them, tending them – even cleaning them out. Above all, she rejoiced in the lovely, warm feeling she felt inside. To think: all these beautiful, heart-fluttering creatures were dependent on her, and her alone. Yet she it was who felt grateful. Grateful for the gift of her "babies", as she called them.

However, space was increasingly becoming a headache. The spare bedroom and the small box-room were now completely lined with cages. In addition, she had two cages in her bedroom, one on the landing, one at the bottom of the stairs, two in the passageway alongside the stored furniture, and one in the little porch just inside the back door. She worried about the two in her bedroom. It wasn't hygienic, she knew. But there was no alternative, it seemed.

"Oh, if only I didn't have that heathen, Flint, taking up the whole parlour!" she yelled, as she walked past his door one day.

And indeed she began to get so desperate that several times she thought of reclaiming her parlour. Or rather, getting the pet shop keeper to do it for her – because she couldn't bring herself to face Flint again.

Then she had an idea. One that changed the picture completely. Such a simple idea, it was. She was surprised she hadn't thought of it before. She would order a shed for the garden. A big one. One that could easily be extended and converted into an aviary for the hardier birds. The more delicate of her babies – those originating from warmer climes – would of course continue to be accommodated in the house.

When it arrived and was erected for her, she was pleasantly surprised to find how big it was. And how light and airy, too, with its little windows, both of which could be opened. As soon as the two men had gone, she stood inside and closed the door.

"Oh, how peaceful it is in here," she said appreciatively, looking out onto the little garden.

She wouldn't ever be without her babies, of course, but even she had to admit they could be rather noisy.

"And how clean and sweet the air smells," she said, breathing in deeply – for she also had to admit that, despite her best endeavours, the atmosphere in her house was sometimes, well, a bit whiffy.

"Yes, how nice it is, just for these few minutes, to stand here quietly by myself." And the better to savour these precious moments,

75

she crossed the garden to the house and carried back one of the easy chairs from the passage.

"Yes, so quiet and relaxing," she murmured, closing the door and sinking into the cushioned comfort of her chair.

As she sat there, luxuriating in her new surroundings, enjoying her few snatched minutes of peace, time seemed to stand still. In fact, she remained in her little haven for over half an hour – just sitting, most of the time. Just sitting with her eyes closed. Then suddenly a rather daring thought came to her.

"Why not!" she cried, jumping to her feet. "Just till Harold gets back from his holidays – and till I can drag him away from his allotment." Harold was her odd-job man. "Yes, why not move my bed in here?"

Her mind was immediately active. She would need a little cupboard of some sort for her clothes. And a few books and other bits and bobs. Not much else, really – except perhaps her dad's old primus stove.

"Yes," she said, again talking out loud to herself as she so often did, "the stove's a very good idea. Set me up nicely, it will. A cup of tea, first thing. Before I go to say good morning to my babies."

The more she thought about it, the more convinced she was. "Why, it'd be like camping out," she said to herself, excitedly. "And less chance of psittacosis," she added, thinking of something she had read recently.

More importantly, it would create more space for the birds inside the house. The cages in the passage, along with those at the head and foot of the stairs, could all be moved into her bedroom. She was delighted.

Six weeks went by – six lovely, happy, summery weeks, which saw Charlotte either busy caring for her birds, or relaxing in her new quarters. It was a heavenly period. The little shed, with its bit of garden in front, had become her Eden. Each day, she emerged from her retreat to walk among her birds, talking to them, tending them lovingly – "a bit like St Francis," she would smile – before retiring fatigued for a few blessed hours of peace and contemplation. She was happier than she had been for years.

But it was Charlotte's nature to brood on things. Was it not rather unfair that while she lay, night after night, enjoying the comfort of her new quarters, her little babies in the house across the garden were living in over-crowded cages? Even after the little aviary was built, wouldn't some of her birds have better living conditions than others? And she thought again of those words from Genesis, chapter one, verse 20: "And God said, let the waters bring forth abundantly the moving creature that hath life, and fowl that may fly above the earth in the open firmament of heaven."

Nancy – who had strong views about keeping birds in cages – had once quoted this passage at her, adding pointedly, "And 'in the open firmament', remember? That's what God said. Need I say more?"

Loath though she was to concede that her friend might have had a point, Charlotte couldn't stop fretting about it. The tiresome woman had touched a nerve.

So right away, in the middle of the night, she let herself into the house and set about opening cages, one after another, until every bird in the house had the option to fly freely in its own room. Not in the open firmament, true – she knew she couldn't go that far: they wouldn't survive for more than a few minutes in the wild – but now, one and all, they could each use their wings as God intended, for proper flight. Those upstairs would now have the run of their rooms, while those downstairs would have the run of the passage. The thought pleased her.

There would be a lot of mess, of course; she realized that. But she would clear it up. And in any case, what did it matter? She was sure her loving parents, looking down on her from above, would approve. In the old days, before first Mam then Dad became poorly, the house had been such a happy place. And what had it become now? Little better than a prison, really – though in truth this was the first time she had thought of it this way. Feelings of guilt, she supposed. Mainly about Captain Flint. Thanks to Nancy, she had fretted over the other birds; but Flint's confinement in the foul cell that used to be her lovely parlour had troubled her more than she had been willing to admit. He had brought it on himself, of course, but she still felt bad about it. So much so that now, for two pins, she would release him as well, except – *no, dear God, perish the thought!* – she knew the harm he would surely do to her little ones in the passage. Yes, she had to put Flint out of her mind. She was doing the right thing; she was sure of it. Indeed, she felt better already. Yes, she felt cleaner, clearer of conscience, as she dropped into bed. She was exhausted. Mentally and physically. But now she could sleep untroubled.

It was mid-afternoon before she came round.

"Oh, my Lord," she cried, when she read the time on her father's little travelling clock. She had slept the clock round. "How lazy can you get!" And she shot out of bed. "My babies, my babies!" There was no time to lose; her birds needed fresh food and water. "Dear Lord, I'm neglecting my babies!"

She dressed hurriedly, and within two or three minutes she was crossing the garden to start her chores.

"Morning, my beauties," she called out, as she reached to open the back door. "Mammy's here. Sorry I'm – "

She stopped mid-sentence, suddenly aware of a noisy clamour and commotion coming from inside the house.

"Dear Jesus!" she cried out in alarm, as she opened the door a few cautious inches and sidled through the narrow opening. "Whatever is going – "

She broke off to close the door quickly behind her. She couldn't have moved any faster, but despite this she had felt a fluttering draught against her face and legs as several birds beat a frantic path to freedom. Now her alarm turned to fear.

The air was alive with birds! Scores and scores of them, of all sizes and colours, flying wildly about in the passage and up and down the staircase. Everywhere she looked, everywhere she went, there were birds darting, diving, gliding, landing, taking off, cheeping, whistling, croaking, squawking. The din was appalling; the smell of droppings, stifling. She felt dizzy and sick, as it dawned on her how this chaos might have come about.

"Oh, you stupid woman!" she cried, as she began to make her way up the stairs to the bedrooms. As if to confirm her blunder, one of her precious lovebirds flew towards her and landed in her hair, scratching her scalp before it could free itself.

She knew what she would find. In the heady excitement of liberating her babies she had carelessly – *no, negligently!* – forgotten to close the bedroom doors behind her. And now the inmates were flying everywhere in the house, mixing with other birds – birds of different sizes; different species, even, so she couldn't be sure they wouldn't injure or even kill one another. And such chaos! She doubted whether order could ever again be restored.

"How could you?" she berated herself, as she fled tearfully down the stairs. "One small lapse, one silly mistake – and now all this."

At the bottom of the staircase, just as she turned into the passage, she slipped on a mess of droppings and fell heavily, knocking her head against the door to the parlour. A loud, protesting shriek came from within.

"Ah, the pirate wants his breakfast, does he?" she cried. "I see. ." She picked herself up and yelled at the door. "Well, hard lines, Flint! No longer top priority, I'm afraid. And serves you right, too."

She made her way back along the passage towards the outside door. Her progress was slow. Birds were winging round her in a frantic swarm, some banging into her and clinging to her clothing. Two landed

79

in her hair and a third crashed into her face. More and more birds surrounded her, and several effected a landing. She tried to brush them off, but they clung desperately to her clothing. They scratched and clawed and nipped her uncovered parts in such a frenzied fashion that she was almost led to think the unthinkable. Surely her birds – her babies, whom she loved more than anything or anybody, apart from the Lord Jesus, of course – did not intend any harm? No, of course not. They were just confused by the chaos, that was all.

When she reached the outside door, she saw that the kitchen door opposite was almost covered by a heaving swarm of birds. Others were diving in, trying to join the throng. It was as if they were trying to gain access.

"Strange," she said to herself, as she extricated yet another bird from her hair. "Can't be thirst. Too soon, I would have thought. But they're going to need water before long. Perhaps they know? Can sense it? I must get to the taps."

More by touch than sight, she found the door handle and let herself into her little kitchen. Ever since she had billeted herself in the shed this room had been the only no-go area of the house, and it was just as she had left it: refreshingly clean and tidy. But not for long! Not for more than a second.

What happened next took her totally by surprise. It was as if a vacuum had existed in her kitchen, so that when the door was opened all the birds clamouring outside – indeed every bird in the house, it seemed – were sucked into that tiny space. The room was suddenly thick, palpably thick, with a swarming mass of wings, feathers, beaks and claws. She found herself covered in birds. Painfully, frighteningly covered. And her light clothing offered no protection against their grappling claws. She was almost pulled down by the combined weight of them, but she managed at last to reach the sink and turn the taps full on.

80

To get back to the outside door, she decided to drop down to floor level. It was calmer down there – below the tumult, below the base of the fluttering cloud. Almost peaceful by comparison. She paused for a moment or two, gathering strength, before setting off on her hands and knees. By the time she reached the outside door, passing several fallen birds along the way, she was close to exhaustion and covered in blood from dozens of tiny wounds.

Several birds escaped with her as she let herself out of the side door. It surprised her that she no longer minded. They were off to fly freely in the open firmament of heaven, as God intended.

"Maybe they won't last long," she said to herself, consolingly, "but they'll enjoy a few moments of freedom. It's a brief enough life for us all. Birds and humans, alike. So fly, little babies, fly."

One thing remained for her to do before she retired to her shed. She went round to the coal bunker, now serving as a feed store, and lifted out several sacks of seed and nuts. Two at a time, she dragged them to the side door. She slit each one with the garden spade before opening the door and pushing it inside. Again, a few birds escaped in the process.

"Good luck," she cried after them. "Enjoy." And through the door she called to those inside. "Same for you. Be happy. Rejoice in the freedom of the house."

Two Sundays later, on her way to church, Nancy stopped for a moment outside Charlotte's house. There was nothing to be seen through the parlour window, apart from a gaudy, upside-down parrot hanging from the curtains. It gave her quite a turn at first.

"A plaything, obviously," she said to herself, recovering her composure. "Some cheap and nasty toy, bought to amuse that heathen, Joseph, no doubt."

A little higher up the building, it was a different story. The space behind the glass of the front bedroom window appeared to be heaving with fluttering wings. Some of the birds, frantic to get out it seemed, were diving repeatedly at the glass. Even through the double-glazing, Nancy could hear the din they were creating.

"Oh, dear God, what's going on?" she cried out loud. "Another Babylon, by the look of things. Surely she's never given them the run of the house?" And she brought to mind, as she crossed the road and moved on, some words from Revelations: "a habitation of devils ... a cage of unclean birds".

Oh, the foolish creature, she thought. I must drop in after the service and give her a talking to. She'll have to get rid of them. End this nonsense. It's gone too far. Such a nice little house, it used to be. In the old days. When Martha and Henry were alive. Always so clean and tidy. Always so peaceful.

Two hours later, as good as her word, she was knocking on Charlotte's front door. After waiting two or three minutes without a response, she took the little path along the side of the house. As she passed the outside door, the din from inside was frightening.

"Like Dante's Inferno!" she uttered, as she carried on to the back garden.

It was the same at the rear of the house. Through the kitchen window, and the windows of the spare bedroom and the box room, clusters of birds could be seen clinging to the tattered curtains, while dozens of others were milling about and flying in at the glass. There must have been hundreds of them, she estimated.

God alone knows what it must be like inside, she thought. The noise, and the mess. The stench, too, presumably. Surely Charlotte wasn't living in that hideous chaos?

She banged on the kitchen window, and then on the side door, several times, but it soon became obvious that she was wasting her time. Even if Charlotte was in there, she wouldn't hear anything with all that din going on.

She tried the side door. To her surprise, it was unlocked. Slowly, she turned the handle and opened the door an inch or two. Instantly, several birds flew out, one of them scratching her face as it made its frantic dash for freedom. She snapped the door shut again. This was a job for the authorities, she realized.

She was on the point of leaving when she thought she caught a movement through the window of the little shed across the garden. She went to investigate. The door appeared to be locked; so she stepped across to the window. Standing on her tip-toes, she peered in through the dirty glass.

Charlotte was perched on the edge of a chair, her trunk rocking – almost swinging – backwards and forwards, her head twitching left and right, up and down, in a series of small jerky movements. She was filthy. Her hair had matted into a sort of wild crest on the top of her head, and the bare parts of her body were covered in what appeared to be small feathers.

"What the …?" began Nancy under her breath, pressing her face closer to the glass. "No – that's ridiculous, surely?"

But they looked like feathers. Small ones, at least. Or perhaps wisps of down? They appeared to be stuck to her skin; either that, or they were trapped in the scabs of the cuts and scratches that scarred her body.

Around her feet, which were grey and bare, there were scraps of food lying in a pool of fluid. To her left there was a small mound of birdseed, in which two small birds nestled as they fed. Two or three other birds – they looked like sparrows – could be seen winging about the room from time to time. There were clothes and old newspapers strewn everywhere. Nancy swallowed hard. The place was positively squalid.

On the low table beside Charlotte was a bucket, served by a length of hose that snaked along the floor to the side of the shed. For a moment, she stopped rocking and dipped a dirty hand into the bucket.

She pulled it out and drank – or rather, sucked – from her cupped palm. Then she continued to rock, and to perform again the strange little darting movements of her head.

At one point, she looked across at the window. She seemed to recognize the face peering in at her – or, at least, she appeared to register that she was being observed. However, all she did was smile. It was an odd little smile, made by fractionally parting her pale, beaky lips. Then she started singing to herself. Or trilling, more like. It was a strange noise; one that synchronized with her rhythmical rocking.

After a couple of minutes, she paused to reach out her hand again, this time to tinkle a little china bell that lay next to the water bucket. Nancy recognized it at once as the one Martha, Charlotte's mother, used to have in her bedroom to summon assistance.

Charlotte tinkled it again. Her beaky smile broadened at the sound of her little plaything. She recommenced her rocking; she resumed her trilling. She did not appear agitated. On the contrary, there was an air of contentment about her, almost as if – there in her messy cell, shut away from the world – she had found a kind of peace, a kind of freedom.

THE FALLING MAN

It was back. The image of the falling man.

Perhaps it had never been away? Despite the dramatic events of the last twenty-four hours, perhaps it had never been dismissed: merely relegated?

It was the dream that had brought it back, he was sure of that. Such a weird dream. Like nothing he had ever experienced before: like nothing, he hoped, he would ever experience again.

He had read somewhere that dreams were little more than the disposal of neural waste. Well, this one had been a right rubbish tip, a real rag-bag, and no mistake. He could see where some of it had come from; but the rest was nightmarish. In places, it was more like something out of Revelations.

The last few scenes were unbearable. He was underground suddenly, tumbling, somersaulting again and again along a narrow tunnel, then thrown out into a vast cavern with dark recesses, from which phantasmagoric creatures were leaping out. Hideous creatures, they were, with long necks and twin, lolling heads whose maws were running with blood and slime; and their breath was foul and not just hot, but fiery, singeing his flesh. And the creatures were now clawing at his body with such terrifying, scaly talons – the pain making him cry out. He tried to protect himself, but his hand wouldn't move. It seemed to be fastened somehow. Was he paralyzed? He tried again.

"It's all right Mr. Fleming," a voice was saying, answering his cry. "Try to keep still. Don't want to pull the line out, do we? That's better. Yes, I know – you've had a bit of a rough time of it. It was a long operation."

Ah, so that was it? He remembered now: the pain that had doubled him up, made excruciating by each movement of the speeding ambulance. And then the concerned faces, the lights of the theatre.

"Don't worry, you're going to be fine. Just try to lie still. The doctor'll be along in a minute or two to talk to you. She'll tell you all about it. Don't be afraid to press the pain button if it gets too much for you. And don't worry – you can't overdose: it won't let you."

He told the doctor about the nightmare images in his dream. "That will be the morphine," she said. "It affects a lot of people like that."

He resolved to go easy on the button in his palm. Sooner have a bit of pain than another reel of Dante's Hell, he thought. Then she told him about the stoma, explaining what it was and why it wasn't in the best position.

"We went for peritonitis at first," she explained. "With so much pain, it seemed the most obvious. So there's also a wound where the appendix came out. Sorry about that."

He'd never heard of a stoma before – but sure as hell, he'd heard of an ileostomy bag. She told him why it was necessary. A couple of feet of his intestine was now missing, she said. A diseased section had been cut away, and the two joined-together parts needed time to heal.

"So my colon's now a semi-colon?" he quipped.

"Not quite," she smiled. Had she heard the joke before? "But look on the bright side – another couple of hours and it might have been a full stop." Yes, she had.

Was there a bright side to cancer, he was left wondering? The biopsy report had yet to come through, but he was thinking the worst. And if it was cancer, could anyone be sure they'd cut it all away?

Meanwhile, he had six tubes or wires connecting him to somewhere beyond his body, a wound the size of a Caesarean incision, a hole in his belly with a wet nose poking out of it – and, if he ever did manage to walk again, there would be a bag of shit swinging between his legs. He was trying to be positive, he really was. But it was hardly surprising that the image of the falling man had returned. He felt he had fallen a pretty long way himself.

It was a poignant image, the image of the falling man. For him, it was even more haunting than the collapse of the burning Twin Towers, which had been almost too theatrical to take in – like some scene from a disaster movie. In the newspaper photograph, one leg of the falling man was straight, the other flexed at the knee, so that if you turned the image on its side, you saw a position commonly adopted during sleep. Except for the arms. They were held at the side: straight, unseen. Nobody sleeps like that, he had thought.

A member of the newspaper's editorial staff had described the falling figure as looking serene. This could have had nothing to do with its facial features; they were so indistinct that all you might venture was a view that it was probably a man, and that he was dark-skinned. Even families desperate to identify loved ones could make nothing of the face. No, he thought, it was the position of the body that had encouraged the sub-editor's view. That, and a belief held by some, perhaps, that the falling man was heading for a better place.

The image had affected him profoundly. Seen like that, in one still frame, on the front page of the newspaper the following day, it might have been tempting to think serenity. And after all the shock-horror TV coverage, it would indeed have helped some people to think of 'the jumpers' – for the falling figure captured on film was far from being the only one – as falling angels, winging their way to paradise.

Being agnostic, his own response had inevitably been more rational. Forget serenity, he had thought. Yes, it was a lovely idea perhaps – but a silly one, surely? Instead, think physics. Think the gathering speed of a falling body. Dare to think 'thirty-two feet per second, per second'. Dare to think how fast this person – descending from towers over a thousand feet high – would be falling after just four or five seconds. Think of the rush of air. Think of the turbulence pulling at the clothing, pulling at the body, pulling at the corners of the mouth. Imagine a face distorted by these forces. Imagine a face distorted by panic, terror. A face distorted by the fear of impact.

These had been his thoughts; and they were not comfortable ones. They had disturbed him at the time; and as he now knew, they would disturb him again in the future. They came about because, unlike that newspaper's sub-editor, he was able to remind himself that when you looked at such a photograph you were looking at a snap-shot, a frozen fragment of time: a mere instant, captured in one frame. Had you been able to see the falling man a moment before, a moment after, a moment two seconds after that, you would have gained a completely different impression. You would have seen the body in different positions as it tumbled through the air; you would have seen its clothing plucked at, pulled away – possibly even torn – by the turbulence. In short, you would have acquired a much more realistic idea of what it must be like to be somersaulting through the air at breath-taking speed, knowing that you are hurtling to certain death. "Equate that with serenity!" he had protested.

And in turn – for this was another train of thought – equate it with the suggestion, voiced by some, that 'the jumpers' were cowards, taking the easy way out. The easy way out? Personally, he couldn't imagine what it must be like – how desperate you would have to be – to hurl yourself into space, to spend your final few seconds of life plummeting a thousand feet, thinking of that final, hideous, moment of impact.

No, he had maintained, think desperation. Think the most extreme form of 'Hobson's choice': jump – or stay and face being burned alive. Think courage, if you will. Think anything you like – but don't think cowardice. Don't think cowardice, chiefly because – oh, use your imagination, he wanted to shout – some of the so-called jumpers may not have jumped at all. They may have been blasted from the building by explosions. They may have blundered, blinded by smoke, overcome by fumes, towards a draught of fresh air – only to find themselves hurtling through space. They may have been forced out by the press of people behind them. Perish the thought, some indeed may even have been pushed. Not all were suicides, leaping from one inferno to another, destined for eternal damnation, as some members of the Catholic community seemed to suggest. He had found that an appalling notion: quite obscene.

The thought of those poor, desperate people – over two hundred, it was estimated – jumping or falling to their deaths, had preyed on his mind. And behind his thoughts, there was always that haunting image of the falling man. It never appeared again in the newspapers, or on television screens – perhaps because America needed images more heroic than those of people apparently jumping ship – but it was etched ineradicably into his retina, into his visual memory.

He himself had fallen a long way, and fast, during the hours leading up to, and following, his operation. But not at a constant rate. He was for example caught and wafted up when the biopsy revealed that he didn't have cancer: merely something called 'acute diverticulitis'. And again when he was finally discharged from the hospital to begin his rehabilitation programme. But he found himself falling once more when his bossy sister threatened to come and look after him for a few weeks, and again when his bag came adrift in the butcher's while he was buying a bit of mince for a shepherd's pie. Slid down the inside of his trousers, it did, and made a mess on the floor. Mr. Fletcher, looking very concerned, thinking no doubt about his business, had to put sawdust down. A shop full of people, too. It was very embarrassing.

After that, things didn't go too badly for a while. He had settled into a routine; he thought he was coping. Then in quick succession he suffered a pulmonary embolism and a DVT. Although the embolism was alarming, making breathing very painful for a couple of weeks, the symptoms were short-lived. The thrombosis was another matter entirely. Not only did it leave him initially with a leg as thick and as heavy as a tree trunk, making walking difficult, it left him dependent on anti-coagulant drugs. More seriously, it meant that his ileostomy couldn't be reversed for at least another nine months – and, worst of all, it left him too weak to resist his sister, Hilda, who now moved in and took control of his life. For the next few weeks he didn't just fall, he plummeted, almost hitting rock-bottom.

What saved him temporarily was a violent bust-up with his sister, the outcome of which was that she left him "to stew in his own juice", as she put it. And he did – almost literally. He lived out of tins – often not even bothering to heat the contents – and he frequently neglected to shave and take a bath. No domestic routine was observed. His little house rapidly became a tip.

Unsurprisingly his physical health deteriorated. Not only that, he became subject to alarming mood swings. During one of these, he physically evicted a poor woman who had been sent by Social Services to assess his situation. This wasn't in character at all; he had been such a gentle, courteous man. But things were to get even worse.

One day a little girl from along the road – Kelly, she was called – wandered into his house through the open door. It was a hot day, and she was thirsty. He gave her a drink of orange juice. "Such a sweet girl," he thought. Unlike other visitors, she seemed oblivious of the chaotic state of the place – and indeed of his unkempt appearance. She laughed a lot at his little jokes and seemed quite relaxed in his company; she appeared not to mind his odd mannerisms. It turned out that she loved reading. No surprise, then, that when she saw all the bookshelves in his front room, her little face lit up. "Just like a library!" she cried.

He gave her a book to read. She took it away, delighted. The following day she appeared in his house again: she had come, she said, "to change the library book". This had tickled him. He was delighted with her; delighted to have an eager pupil once again: delighted with pleasurable human contact. He found her another book; drawing on his experience, it was one that he knew would be just as suitable.

"Will you read to me?" she asked suddenly. "I'd like that. Mammy reads to me sometimes. But not Daddy. He's never in at bedtime. Will you – please?"

And before he knew it, she had hopped onto his knee and had leaned back, eyes closed, head on his chest, ready to be entertained. He started to read. She was still for a while, then she shuffled about on his lap, as if trying to get a more comfortable position. Soon she was still again, and for the next five minutes they were both transported. He had not known such simple contentment for months.

Then suddenly – so suddenly that she knocked the specs from his nose, the book out of his hands – she shot up, pushed him away abruptly, and ran out of the house.

He didn't know what to make of her unceremonious exit. But he thought no more about it – until that evening, when there was a knock on his door. It was the police, and he was taken away for questioning. Sweet little Kelly – he still found it hard to believe – had run home to her mother, and had accused him of what one of the detectives referred to euphemistically as "inappropriate behaviour".

Protesting his innocence, he gave his side of the story. They ignored his protestations.

"Is it true," one of them said, "that little girls arouse you? You know – that their close presence gives you pleasure? Enough to get you going?"

"Certainly not," he said. "I don't know what you mean. Reading was the only pleasure we shared."

"Ah," the second one persisted, "so little Kelly was lying, was she, when she told her Mummy that she had felt something "big and firm and warm" – her words, Mr. Fleming, not mine – beneath your trousers?"

"God – no!" he cried. "The poor child – is that what she thought? No, she wasn't lying." The detectives looked triumphant. "But you ... she. . . you've all misunderstood. What she felt was my ileostomy bag."

His medical records were checked. Charges were not pressed. But the police were not really convinced, he could tell, and he was cautioned never to invite little girls into his house again. He was also informed that the incident would be recorded.

So, on top of everything else, he now had a police record! Not to mention being treated like a pariah by his neighbours. The word 'pervert' was carried on the wind, whispered among the street litter. 'There was no smoke without fire,' it was said. They all agreed.

He now descended into a deep depression, one from which he could not seem to lift himself. But he still had a good way to fall. Three months later, he was apprehended by a security officer as he was attempting to leave Marks and Spencer's with three pairs of jockey shorts he hadn't paid for. He didn't wear jockey shorts, for goodness sake – so what was he doing leaving the store with three pairs of the bloody things? He couldn't say; he seemed vague. 'Conveniently absent-minded', the police called it. They hadn't forgotten him. They could do without 'pilfering perverts' on their patch, he was told. So he was charged, brought up before the magistrate, and promptly given a six months' suspended sentence.

His memory of events after that was scant and uncertain. There was someone from the Health Authority – or was it Social Services: he couldn't be sure – tut-tutting about the mess his house was in. He remembered that. Oh, yes – and Hilda had appeared at some point: whether before, or later, he couldn't say. Oddly, she was wearing a white face mask, he seemed to remember – but maybe this was just his imagination? There was a ride somewhere, too. In a big vehicle, like an ambulance. Perhaps he was being taken to hospital again. He couldn't be sure.

The Home was called 'The Pines' – which was odd, he thought later, once he had begun to unscramble his brain, because there wasn't a pine tree to be seen anywhere near the place. But it wasn't so bad. He had his own little room, up on the second floor. Quite a good view, too. Over the rooftops he could see into the Arboretum. And there were no bars at the windows. He remembered thinking that, early on, and feeling relieved. "Thank goodness it wasn't that sort of establishment," he thought. He had begun to wonder.

No, it wasn't so bad. A bit pokey. Just a bed, a bedside locker and a built-in wardrobe. Plus a bookcase, of course. There had been resistance, but he had insisted. At least he had some of his favourite books around him. What had happened to the rest, he wasn't sure. Perhaps he would ask Hilda the next time she came. Perhaps not. She seldom came these days, anyway. He had some mercies to be thankful for, it seemed.

The only real drawback to the place was the lack of stimulating company. Most of the other inmates – no, *guests*; or, these days, perhaps *clients?* – were much older, some in their eighties and nineties. Many were infirm. Some were no longer 'with it', as one of the care staff put it; they spent most of their time staring vacantly into space – come to think of it, a bit like he himself must have been until recently – and being carried from one place to another. Hopefully, he thought, they were at least incapable of contemplating their future.

He spent a lot of time in his room. Reading, mostly. But sometimes just lying on his bed, looking at the ceiling, thinking. Occasionally he would look out towards the Arboretum. Either way – thinking, or just looking – he was grateful. He thought he had stopped falling.

He was about to be proved wrong. Having little else to think about, the image of the falling man began to insinuate itself again. At first, he didn't mind. He felt he could relate to it even more closely now – now that he knew what it was like to go into freefall. He had experienced

93

some of the panic – the terror, indeed – that can arise from that sensation of plummeting out of control.

Or had he? No, of course he hadn't. How could anyone fully understand what those poor devils must have been feeling in those last few seconds before death? Supposing they were thinking anything at all, that is. For it occurred to him – had it been stupid of him not to think of it before – that they might have lost consciousness at some point, falling from that height, and at such a phenomenal speed. Perhaps, mercifully, after a few seconds, you just blacked out and hit the ground knowing nothing. But he would never know, would he? For one thing, in this country, there wasn't anywhere high enough, was there? It could never be put to the test.

Increasingly, the image of the falling man began to haunt him. He thought about it more and more – to the point that he thought of little else. He became obsessed by the plight of 'the jumpers' and the nightmare they had gone through. It began to affect him physically. He went off his food; he neglected his appearance; he failed to observe the simple routines of the institution. He was falling once again. The staff became concerned – so concerned that they contacted his sister.

Then one day, soon after this, their anxieties appeared to be justified. He failed to come down for breakfast; and despite an extensive search of the house and its grounds, he was nowhere to be found. He had gone missing. Moreover, matron had found a copy of his will lying, neatly laid out, on his bed. The police were informed; another telephone call was made to Hilda; local residents were asked to look out for him.

Had he been there to observe it, the hue and cry would have amused him; he had always had a passion for drama. But at the moment, surprisingly, he was not stirred by anything; he was quite calm. It was true that he had made up his mind quite suddenly – one minute he was reading Saturday's paper, the next he was letting himself out through the side door, the one used by the staff when they

94

went on and off duty – but he felt composed now. He knew exactly what he was going to do.

It was a Bank Holiday, and the warm sunshine had drawn out the crowds. As he walked towards the outskirts of town there were people everywhere, laughing, chattering, promenading slowly, leisurely – just happy to be free of normal workday routines, seemingly content in ignorance of the knowledge he was about to acquire. Why did he find that strange?

In the lift, as he went up and up and up, with time to dwell on things, he did have one moment of doubt and insecurity. Supposing it proved not to be high enough to offer conclusive proof? All this, in vain? Then he pulled himself together. It wasn't *as* high; of course it wasn't. But he was sure it was high enough.

It certainly felt high enough, out there on the parapet, looking down at the dwarfed holiday-makers below. But it didn't do to look down. The falling man probably had to tell himself just that. "Don't, whatever you do, look down," he may have said, steadying himself. "Too unnerving. No, just go for it."

FOLLOWING BALLOONS

Such a nice man. Maybe I was worrying for nothing?

The school had set up the meeting. Concerned about my friends, they said. I couldn't understand it. I didn't have any friends. Not that kind, anyway. That was the problem, they said. Not for me, I said. I was quite happy as I was.

It was my Dad who took me, of course. My Mam's an actress. Not famous, or anything. You won't have heard of her. Works at some theatre. In Leeds, I think. Small parts, mainly. But while she's working in one play, she's often rehearsing for the next – so she's always either acting or rehearsing. Never has the time to take me anywhere. It's always down to my Dad. He's a musician: a bassoonist. Teaches part-time. Goes from school to school. "Very pathetic," he tells people, and then he laughs as if it's all a big joke. I don't get it.

My Dad often says things I don't get. Take this man we went to see. I heard my Dad say he was a trick cyclist – which I know can't be right, because you should have seen the size of him! Huge, he was. At least, the top half of him was. Large, round head. Big fat belly, stretching his belt. I thought he would burst his trousers! But he had these short, spindly legs. He looked so top heavy, it made me laugh. I couldn't see *him* riding a bike. He'd always be falling off! Perhaps that was his trick – staying on? Nice man, though. Henderson, I think he was called. Very smiley face. Not quite sure who he was. Not a doctor, I don't think. No white coat. And nothing round his neck for listening to chests with. Seemed very interested in Mam for some reason. Could he have seen her on the stage, I wondered?

"Now, tell me about your little friends," he said, once he got going. "Why so many? What is it about them that attracts you?"

"Well," I told him, "I like the shape of them. I like their big, round faces. Faces you can trust. Like moons, they are. Especially those that float near the ceiling. I can look up, and there they are – my very own full moons. And they're so smooth and soft. I often reach out and stroke them. Those I keep tied close to the floor, I mean. I like the smell of them, as well." I paused. I had to be careful. I could feel myself starting to bubble over. It always happened when I was asked to talk about my friends. It wouldn't do to get over-excited. Not everyone understood. The nice man seemed to understand, though. He was smiling all over his own round face, encouraging me to go on. "And one of the nicest things about them is that they're there – all around me – but they're quiet. They don't speak till they're spoken to. I like that."

"So they *can* speak, then?" I sensed he was getting excited now.

"Oh, yes – when I want them to. I can get them to talk."

"And how do you do that?"

"Simple," I said. "I draw my fingers across their skin and sort of pinch them. That soon sets them off. That soon gets their squeaky voices going."

"And you can understand what they're saying?"

"Of course," I said. Was he stupid, or something? "Be no point if I couldn't, would there?"

"Of course not." The nice man's face grew even smilier. "Thank you, Kelvin – that's very interesting." He looked down at some notes on his slippery knee. "And how many of these little friends have you got, may I ask?"

"Scores," my Dad answered. I wondered how long it would be before he chipped in. A broad grin filled the space between his bassoon-blowing cheeks. "Hundreds of them, all floating about. Like clouds. Yes – head forever in the clouds, my boy. That right, Kelvin?" I nodded. "Yes – all over the house, they are. In every room. But mainly in his bedroom. You should see them in there. All bobbing about. You can't get stirred for them. Not that we mind. It's his room. Other rooms, though – that's a different matter. The kitchen, for example. Wouldn't do to have them in there, now would it? Not the helium ones, anyway." He paused to laugh at his little joke. I'd heard it before. "Yes – we've got hundreds. Different sizes, different colours, different materials. Singles, doubles, clusters. Balloon mad, he is. Always has been, ever since he was a small child – well, a baby, really."

"Really?" The nice man was getting excited again. "Since he was a baby? Now that *is* interesting. Can you remember when it all started?"

"I can actually," my Dad said. "The very day, in fact. Twelfth Night, it was. I was taking down the decorations. Broke off to read him his bedtime story. I thought he'd gone to sleep – even before I'd finished – but he must've crept downstairs to the sitting room, the little monkey, and smuggled them upstairs. He'd only be about eighteen months at the time – and there he was, lying fast asleep, his head resting between two white balloons. They'd gone down a bit by then – but even so, they could have burst. He'd have got a nasty shock then, eh? And bits of rubber lying about? He might've choked on those."

"Yes, I can still remember those balloons," I said. "The feel of them – so warm and soft and smooth against my lips. They were lovely, those two."

"Your mother didn't think so!" my Dad said. "She was cross – cross with the pair of us – when she heard about it."

"She wasn't there, then?" Mr. Smiley asked.

"No, she was at the theatre. Doing *Twelfth Night,* as a matter of fact." Dad laughed. "She was hardly ever in at evening time. We were used to that, weren't we, Kelvin?"

"Yes – but it was lovely when she *was* at home," I said.

"I'm sure," said Mr. Smiley. "Love your mother, do you, Kelvin?"

"I'll say!" I cried. "She's lovely. No, not just lovely – beautiful! Everybody says so. She's an actress, you know."

"Yes, so your father tells me." Mr. Smiley nodded, and his eyes twinkled. "Miss her, do you?"

"Yes. Or I used to, when I was little. Missed her a lot, then. Especially at bedtimes. Dad's great. Tells really good stories. But he smells of whisky and fags." I looked across at him and gave him a big smile "and he's very hairy! Mam was never hairy, of course." The thought of a hairy Mam suddenly made me laugh. "No – always soft and smooth, she was. And when she leaned over to kiss me goodnight, she always smelled nice."

"I can imagine," said Mr. Smiley, beaming at me. Then he turned to my Dad. "Well – all those balloons! I'm trying to imagine. Perhaps I could see for myself?"

And he did see for himself. He came two Saturdays later, in the afternoon. A 'home visit', he called it. My Mam couldn't be there, of course. Doing a matinee. Mr. Nice-and-Smiley seemed disappointed, I could tell. Perhaps he had once seen her on stage? Perhaps he was a fan? But when he saw my collection, he soon looked smiley again. His eyes opened wide with amazement. Wide and round and shiny. A bit like my balloons.

"Wow!" he said, bobbing underneath them. "So many!" he said, weaving in and out of them. "Wonderful!" he cried, as he lost himself in the jungle of them.

"And not just balloons. . ." He was admiring my things on the wall. Pictures, mostly. Hot-air balloons, and the men who invented them. But other bits and pieces, as well. For instance, I had a saucer decorated with red, white and blue balloons. Bought it in a shop in Kirkbymoorside. Bought a fan in there as well – you know, one of those things you waft about, to cool yourself with? – with a man holding a string of balloons painted on it. Mr. Smiley seemed very interested in my pictures. Going back to them, he pointed at one and gave me one of his big smiles. "Ah, Montgolfier – yes?"

99

"Yes – but which one?" I knew I had him there. "There were two of them, you see. They were brothers. Joseph-Michel and Jacques-Etienne. That one is Etienne. Everybody seems to remember their last name. And everybody says, "Yes – the first hot air balloon." But they're wrong. It was only the first to carry people. The very first was launched by a man called Pilatre De Rozier. It stayed in the air for fifteen minutes – and it carried a sheep, a duck and a rooster! Bet you didn't know that?"

"You bet right," laughed Mr. Smiley. He turned and stepped closer to my Dad. He dropped his voice, but I could still catch what he was saying. "Very impressive. Your boy knows his stuff. But all this ballonabilia! I mean, we all like balloons, I guess. No harm in that. We tend to associate them with parties, don't we? And therefore with play, with gaiety, with frivolity. But this?" He swept his arm sideways and several balloons bobbed up and down, caught in the draught. "This is something else. Serious stuff. I've never observed anything quite like it. Not just a collector, our Kelvin, is he? Knows the science – the maths, the physics. Knows the history. Knows his subject inside-out."

"You could say that!" Dad laughed. "Never puts his mind to anything else. That's why they're concerned about him at school. But one thing leads to another, that's what I say. I'm not worried. Far from it. He's a bright boy. I think he'll go far." He paused and gave me a smile. "Oh, I know what people think. And yes, it must seem a bit weird. But no harm in that, eh? Chip off the old block, in that respect." He laughed. "I mean, look at me. Spend hours and hours every week with a great big pipe in my mouth – and never an ounce of baccy in it!" He laughed again. "Yes, bassoonists, balloonists – all a little crazy. A bit balloonery, a bit bassoonery, a bit buffoonery, the lot of them!"

That was my Dad all over. Always using big, long words. Loved them, he did. Loved the sound of them, he said. "Like music," he would say. I reckon he made them up, most of them. Good at making

100

things up, my Dad. I wish he hadn't said that, though. You know – used the 'crazy' word? He used it a lot when I was little. Something like it, anyway. "You're daft, me duck, you follow balloons; you wear your father's pantaloons!" – that" s what he used to say. In a sing-song sort of voice. I didn't mind it much when I was little. In fact, it made me laugh. He was always coming out with funny little rhymes. Just trying to make me laugh, really. He meant no harm. But balloons aren't daft. They're fun. And people explore in them. Take them up high – much higher than Mount Everest. And they go round the world in them. They even race in them. Balloons are used in science, as well. They can tell things about the weather. So I hate that rhyme now. When I was little, my Mam used to say, "Call back to him. Tell him – you're the one who's daft, me duck; you're the one who follows bassoons!" But I never did.

When Mr. Smiley left, I went back to my room. My Dad saw him back to his car. My window was open a little bit. Not too much – draughts make my balloons go giddy: throw their strings into a right tangle! – but it was open enough for me to hear them talking on the drive. Words drifted up to me. Like gas-filled balloons. Nice balloon-words, some of them. But some were words I didn't want to hear.

impressive …. that workshop! …. amazing …. privilege to see it ….. those model hot-air balloons ….. quite a flotilla ….. built to scale, you say? – and they actually work? ….. he can make them fly? ….. yes. phenomenal – but worrying ….. not just a harmless bit of balloonmania ….. we're talking obsession here ….. serious already ….. could become dangerous if not treated ….. such a nice boy ….. don't want to see him in an institution, do we? ….. another session, yes ….. thorough examination ….. get your wife to come if she can ….. she could be the key ….. next Thursday all right – at three?

He was wrong there! I don't know what he meant by 'the key' – but whatever it was, my Mam couldn't be it. She couldn't be anything – for the simple reason that she's dead! I've been lying about her. Not the actress bit. You can check that out. But she died when I was three. Suicide, they said. We were living in Canada then. Found in the river, she was, with reeds in her mouth and stones in her pockets. Like Ophelia, Dad said – but I didn't get what he meant. Mam would've got it, he said. I didn't get that, either. Not long after she died, we came to England.

We often pretended she was still alive, Dad and me. I don't know why. It helped, though – you know, in the early days, when I knew she wasn't coming home from rehearsals? Dad started it. It made things easier, he said. It helped to pretend. But pretending wasn't going to help me now. I thought at first that Mr. Smiley was on my side. Now I wasn't so sure. An *institution*, he said. I'm not daft. I know what that means. Big place, with lots of rooms. Like a prison. And me, all alone. None of my friends to keep me company. I couldn't bear that. *Next Thursday*, he said. So I hadn't got long. But a plan was already forming in my mind. Yes, I knew what I had to do. It was dangerous, but it was better than being locked up in a home somewhere.

I had done it before. Well, Dad and me had. When Pythagoras died. Pythagoras was our cat. Well, not really ours. He was a stray; we adopted him. Strange animal, he was, with eyes that didn't match and a broken tail that looked like a bent elbow. Funny name. Dad gave it to him. Anyway, when he died we strapped him into his basket, tied two helium balloons at each end of it, and let him float off high into the sky till he disappeared. It was a great send-off. His *Ascension*, Dad called it, as we watched him going slowly upwards towards the clouds. Then Dad laughed like a drain, saying that somebody, somewhere, was in for a bit of a shock when Pythagoras came down to earth again and made his *Second Coming!* He said some funny things, my Dad.

Pythagoras was skinny. Four balloons were quite enough to see him off. I would need more. Lots more. I tried to work it out. I was a good eight times his weight, so I'd probably need about thirty-five. Maybe half-a-dozen really big ones. Six-footers. I'd have to buy those; and some more helium. There's this shop I go to, when we go into York. I could sneak off there one day. The rest of the cluster could be all different sizes. I'd need some of the smaller ones to burst if I was going too high – and to get ready for landing, of course – and some bottles of water for ballast, to throw overboard if I wasn't going high enough. I'd need some sort of harness, as well. But one of our folding deckchairs would do, I thought. I could strap myself into that.

Planning all this, I got really excited. What an adventure! I always said I would try cluster ballooning when I was bigger – and here I was, a bit earlier than I thought, making my dream come true. Well, maybe ... with a bit of luck! Taking after one of my heroes, as well. 'Lawnchair Larry'. That was his nickname. He was an American. Went up to 16,000 feet, using forty-five weather balloons fastened to his garden chair. How brave was that? Once I got up there, perhaps I could drift across to America and visit Larry? If he's still alive, that is. Need to catch the right winds, though. You can't steer clusters, you see. All you can do is find a good wind. They're big on cluster ballooning in America. I could learn a lot there. Maybe make a name for myself? Become a famous balloonist? Then I'd get back to England. Back to Dad. Dad'll be all right, mind. You know – while I'm away? He's got his fags and his booze – and his music, of course. He'll be happy bassooning while I'm happy ballooning. Hey – that sounds like him talking!

I launched my cluster while Dad was rehearsing with the Theatre Royal orchestra. He had no idea what was going on. Nothing unusual in that. I could do anything I liked. He would have no idea that I had nicked his holiday money to pay for the extra kit. Well – not for ages, he wouldn't. I think he forgets he's got it. Doesn't really need it, you see. We have plenty of money. My Mam left us lots. Got it from her Mam, I think. No, Dad just likes the idea of saving up – so every time he gets paid for a private lesson, he puts the money into a big jar. I often dip into it to buy stuff. I think he knows really – but he never says anything. I don't think he cares. And what does it matter, anyway? We never go on holiday. We never go anywhere. Too busy, both of us, doing what we like best. I've never cleaned him out before, mind. Not to worry: I'll pay him back one day. When I'm rich and famous.

"Goodbye, garden!" I cried, as my balloons sailed upwards. I was left dancing about in my chair below the bunches of strings. The speed took me by surprise. Good job the strapping was strong. "Goodbye, House! Goodbye, Lane! Goodbye, Steeple!" and, in less than a minute or two "Goodbye, Malton! Goodbye, Everywhere!"

High above a patchwork of fields, I was now being dragged towards the base of a long cloud. It was shaped like a cigar. Or, yes – like a zeppelin! I knew all about zeppelins. The first one, made by Count von Zeppelin, was very like a huge balloon. It seemed like a good sign. But it was cold and gloomy inside my cloudy zeppelin. Thank goodness I wasn't in it long. Just long enough to make me glad I was wearing my balaclava helmet and my extra pair of trousers.

Above the cloud, I found myself caught in a fast stream of air. I was now travelling more sideways than upwards. But which way? Which way was America? And would my good friends, the balloons, keep me up? Just as worrying – would I be up here for ever? Because I'd heard Dad say: "Good friends, real friends, never let you down." So many questions. Questions with no answers. But for the moment I was alive – really alive! I felt so excited. What an adventure! I was free – free to follow my balloons. And supposing I never came down – or supposing I hurtled down too fast! – well, it was better than being locked away in an institution.

"Don't worry, Dad," I shouted down – down to a ground I couldn't see. "I'll be back. Till then, be happy for me. Thanks for believing in me."

He did believe in me, my Dad. Always said I would go far! Though how far I'm going, and where, I have no idea. Perhaps I'm just going there and back, to see how far it is? That was another one of his little jokes. Maybe it's not such a bad idea. I'll settle for it. I have little choice.

Yes, I was learning, when you follow balloons you have little choice.

THE VICAR

To begin with, sensible people just thought he was different. That's all. We didn't hate him. Of course we didn't. Why would we? In many ways he was just an ordinary chap. Was even seen in the village pub in the early days. Liked a pint, it seemed. Wore odd socks, it was true. And for some reason that nobody quite understood, he always had a bit of white in his collar; hence his nickname: *The Vicar*. That set him apart. He wasn't a real vicar, of course. Fond of quoting the King James Bible, yes. But he was never ordained. Folk round here weren't comfortable with that. There was always going to be suspicion surrounding someone who wasn't quite what he seemed to be. So he was never really accepted as one of the community. For all that, he was harmless enough, we thought. In the beginning.

Kids were afraid of him, mind. And later, people picked up on that. But then, he was a bit weird to look at. He had black brows that sprouted extravagantly above his wild, protruding eyes. Together with a slightly lob-sided smile, this lent him a somewhat sinister look. And the way he dressed — always in black, with a flowing black cloak — added to the impression. No wonder the kids called him Count Dracula. And they would call out this name as he passed by — after he'd gone a safe distance, that is — to which he would sometimes respond, playing them at their own little game, by laughing fiendishly and lolloping off, his raised arms setting his cloak a-flapping. 'Like a bat in the night!' they would cry. And, arms out-stretched, hands clutching the open ends of their coats, they would wheel about in daring imitation. He seemed to take it in good part. There was no sign that he would ever harm any of them. Far from it: on his daily walk to Fairy Hill he would sometimes pass through a group of youngsters playing on

The Green, and he would throw handfuls of sweeties into the air before hurrying on. He was never the Bogeyman some made him out to be.

Of course, living where he lived did him no favours. Surrounded by trees, his big, dilapidated house was always dark, always in shadow. His curtains were never opened, so not a glimmer of light was seen to escape the premises. *The Vicarage*, village folk mockingly called it – not realizing, most of them, that it had indeed been a manse once upon a time, back in Edwardian days when my father was a boy. Now it was an eerie place. But somehow just a little too over-stated. A brooding caricature of a house. Like something off the set in one of those early black-and-white Dickens films.

No one ever saw inside *The Vicarage*. None of the locals, anyway. Except Mrs. Scrivens, of course. She did a bit of cleaning for him during his first few months in the village. But he gave her the sack. 'Just for disturbing his papers while I was dusting,' she claimed. But more likely for feeding the gossip-hungry with tit-bits – most of doubtful provenance – regarding her mysterious employer. That's probably where some of the more fanciful stories about the 'goings-on' at *The Vicarage* originated: from Mrs. Scrivens, initially, with added embroidery from the wild imaginings of her cronies. Mind, this is a small community: all the villagers were probably guilty of a bit of that, myself included. Ever since Mrs. Scrivens's dismissal, of course, no information about the owner's private life, reliable or otherwise, had come from first-hand experience.

This was not to say that, from time to time, people did not see the inside of *The Vicarage*. Indeed, a few were not only invited in: they even stayed awhile. But they were always strangers, city folk; and they never stayed more than a few days, never long enough to make contact with the villagers. They were brought back to the house by The Vicar himself after one of his regular excursions to London. Down-and-outs, they were, all of them: young women and young men he found on the streets, sleeping rough. And he would offer them food and shelter at *The Vicarage* – clothing too, if they needed it – asking nothing in return. Well, that was not quite true. It is said there's no such thing as a free lunch, and sure enough his captive guests were expected to put up with a constant stream of readings from classical poetry and the Bible – 'just because he was in love with the sound of the words; he wasn't religious or anything,' one recounted. Small wonder no one stayed very long.

The Vicar had become a well-known figure in certain East-End fringe communities – where, apparently, the various charity agencies called him simply 'GS': the Good Samaritan. But because he looked and spoke like a minister, I suppose, the down-and-outs themselves usually called him Holy Joe. All of this only came out afterwards, of course. At the time, the villagers would simply witness certain comings and goings: the rest – and there was a lot of tittle-tattle – was left to speculation based on prejudice and mistrust.

Yes, *The Vicar* was different all right. Writing quite a chapter for himself in local folklore, he was. And speaking of writing, it was later revealed that among his many other interests and activities he had for some time been working on a book. Mrs. Scrivens had testified to that, adding in her inimitable way that it was all Greek to her, "all mumbo-jumbo, abracadabra stuff" – which for her wasn't that far from the mark, in that he was preparing what would have been a controversial interpretation of the famous sixteenth-century allegory, *The Fairie Queene*, which had been the subject of his doctorate.

Oh, if only they had known, those ignorant villagers, that they had in their midst not only a mystical seventh son of a seventh son (and therefore said to be gifted with 'second sight'), but a man who took more than a passing interest in the nature and singularities of Urisks, or Little People. And he was a doctor to boot! Dr. Victor James Kirklea to be precise, who, before his breakdown, had been a much-respected university academic. Oh, wouldn't they have had a field day with all of that! *Dr. Who, did you say? Oh, him? Away with the fairies, that one! Just dropped in from Tudor times. In The Tardis, of course. The way he dresses! Like the Lord of the Underworld. Funny sort of chap. Can't understand a word he says. Definitely not one of us. Exterminate! Exterminate!*

However, one day in early June the villagers were given something they could really get their teeth into. Had a proper field day, they did, and no mistake. The Vicar, it seemed, had gone missing! Miss Thring, the postmistress, recalled that he had not passed the Post Office that morning on his usual walk to the top of Fairy Hill; and earlier, the postman, unable to deliver a parcel, had talked of an "eerie silence" surrounding *The Vicarage*. It was the same that evening: no car in the drive; no sign of life; the place deserted. Or so it seemed.

Ordinarily, little would have been made of this – except, on that same day, little Ellie Winters, whose parents ran the village shop, failed to return home from school. The police were called. Questions were asked. All the villagers were interviewed. But no one was detained for long. In my case – retired head of the village school, Rotarian, chair of the Parish Council – it took all of two or three minutes. All fingers were pointing in the same direction, you see. Obviously the two disappearances were not coincidental. Many spoke out, quite openly. And to my shame, none more vehemently than me. Because she was a nice little thing, Ellie. Lovely smile. Had a kind of innocence. Very trusting. I knew the family. Taught her mother. Father came from Wales somewhere, as I remember. Yes, feelings were running high. You could sense it in the air. 'Find The Vicar,' folk were saying, 'and you'll find the child.'

But the police didn't find him. They didn't have to. He came home, large as life, the following evening. He'd been to Oxford, he claimed; to the Bodleian, doing some research – and he returned, bewildered, to find the police swarming like hornets all through his house, everything turned upside-down and inside-out, the floorboards up, the garden probed, and himself under arrest.

They detained him overnight while the search continued – a search not only of his premises, but up there under arc lights on Fairy Hill, where the superstitious amongst us – by far, the majority – never ventured. But they found nothing. Moreover, The Vicar's story was corroborated by the hotel he had stayed in and by university and library staff in Oxford. He was released by lunchtime the following day, much to the disbelief and disgust of everyone in the village.

Hatred of the man quickly intensified. Blind hatred really, it was – for to my knowledge he had never harmed or spoken ill of anyone in the village. *He's weird, that one. It's got to be him.* That was the general view. And once again, to my shame, it was a view I went along with. *Yes, he's weird, all right. Weird – and sly. But he'll slip up. Mark my words. Got to be guilty. Stands to reason. But they'll find him out. They always do.*

But they didn't. Three weeks went by. Little Ellie was still missing. Ideas were running out. Efforts were frustrated. Hopes were fading. Some in the village were getting hysterical. There was even a whisper of holding a Kangaroo Court.

It was Douglas Talisker – retired jeweller; lives in what used to be the smithy, overlooking The Green – who found the body. The day of the summer solstice, it was, in the early morning, when Douglas was out on Fairy Hill walking his dog, *Whisky.*

Fairy Hill (named *Hob's Knoll* on the Ordnance Survey map) is a strange, wooded mound. According to geologists, it was formed by the last Ice Age; but popular belief offers a much less prosaic explanation. Local folk-law and legend proclaims that the knoll was made by dwarfs, elves, goblins – little people of that ilk – seeking to throw a concealing roof of earth over their kingdom. It is an engaging idea; but fanciful though it may sound, it is probably the private belief of many a villager alive today. It dominates our community, you see, that hill. Has

110

done for centuries. Although it's not really very high – 743 feet to be exact – it towers above the village and the surrounding flat farmland; offering protection, some still believe.

Stories about the hill are legion. Passed down from one generation to the next, they have become part of our folk history; part of our collective psyche, almost. Children are told by superstitious parents to give the place a wide berth. *It's their world. Don't disturb it. Don't meddle with what you don't understand.* Yes, I've heard some of these warnings myself. But don't laugh too dismissively. I'm not afraid to go up there, but even a hoary old sceptic like me has to admit that there is something about the place. Something in the air. Something almost tangible. You hear little noises. You think you see things. You can suddenly go cold for no good reason. You never see anybody up there, yet there are signs aplenty that folk have gone before you. You can feel – sometimes very strongly – that you're being watched.

And what greets you when you reach the small clearing at the summit simply adds to the feeling that things magical and mystical might just be possible on Fairy Hill, for the undergrowth and low, twisted branches are festooned with pieces of brightly coloured material; and slender spirals of aluminium foil dance in the breeze; and nestling in the boles of trees you find wax-encrusted candle-holders and tiny plaster images of little creatures, like mice and moles and gnomes and pixies. And here and there you discover votive messages and bits of cloth (called *clouties* in Scottish) tied or pinned to tree-trunks and branches, stemming from the old days when rags would be left to rot in holy places in the hope of cures for illness, and as offerings to local spirits.

This would have been a familiar scene confronting Douglas and his dog; but on this particular occasion Whisky had dropped to his haunches, whining and growling, refusing to move. He had sensed that something was wrong long before Douglas saw the body of The Vicar hanging from an oak branch. A sudden up-draught had caught his

111

black cloak, lifting it to shoulder level, giving him for a moment the appearance of a grotesque Vesper bat.

The police said it was suicide. The poor wretch, they asserted, had been unable to live with his guilt. They wanted the case closed; their lack of progress had become embarrassing. But Ellie's body had not been found. The locals were not persuaded. There were rumblings of murder – of The Vicar being the victim of a midnight lynch mob. It would have been rough justice, yes; but justice all the same, in the eyes of many round here. However, the police were adamant: they could find no evidence for murder.

There were further rumblings. It wasn't suicide, some believed. And it wasn't murder. It was the work of the Little People! It was retribution for the way in which The Vicar had meddled in their affairs, for the way he had made public the secrets of the Faerie Kingdom. *No!* cried others, claiming greater knowledge of the ways of the Urisk, *fairy folk would never take direct, violent action like that.* The real explanation was simple: The Vicar had been spirited away to their middle-Earth realm, as one of their own, leaving behind the body of a changeling.

I prefer this story. Apart from being the most romantic, it is the most charitable. And I am well disposed to be charitable. I always had a soft spot for The Vicar; but beyond that I have a great deal to thank him for. He was always a diversion, you see. Such an obvious target. Even the police were sucked in. Influenced by local feeling, they took their eye off the ball. They weren't as thorough as they should have been. Yes, of course they checked the Register: they weren't that negligent. But they failed to check whether or not any villagers had ever changed their names. It was a fundamental error. None of us, surely, are quite what we seem to be?

She was a nice little thing, Ellie Winters. So soft. So innocent. So trusting.

COME INTO MY PARLOUR

She saw him coming. Saw him a long time before he was able to see her. She was cheating, of course.

It was an ancient device. A common enough form of deception. Not much more than a trick of the light, when you came to think of it. But she loved it. Forget the physics and the mathematics – never her strong points – and forget the elegant engineering, and the aesthetic appeal of a beautifully crafted object: she was operating on a purely emotional level. Like a primitive clutching a fragment of looking glass, she sensed she was dealing in magic. Lifting it to her eye, she became at once an illusionist, a conjuror of images – for she could make small objects large and large objects small. At a touch, she could bring things out of the mist, promote them, give them definition – and at another touch, condemn them to obscurity. She loved the element of jiggery-pokery.

It was heady stuff. Even now, vague feelings were surfacing that she might be flirting with danger; that she might be dabbling with something she couldn't control. But she was not frightened. On the contrary, she revelled in it. If she *was* playing with fire, she was playing with the biggest fire of them all – for it entertained her to think that the light from the sun had travelled ninety-three million miles expressly to be at her service, to aid her little miracle.

He ran every day if he could. Had done for well over twenty years. Just to keep in condition; he wasn't competitive. His running was a form of celebration. For him the appeal had always been as much about bodily sensation, or the beauty of the terrain, or some meteorological phenomenon – an iridescent dew-drop, a magical sunset, a gathering of storm clouds – as about any demonstration of athletic ability. His well-tuned body allowed him not only to move easily over long distances, but also to travel in the mind and the imagination. Sometimes, on exceptional days, the beauty of the landscape and some fluke in the weather would coincide with a peak in his physical condition to create a feeling of well-being so profound that it seemed to touch the very core of him, uplifting not only his spirit but also his feet, affording him a wonderful, weightless feeling, as if he were floating, moving on air.

He had known that it wouldn't be like that today, the twenty-fourth of June: the tenth anniversary of poor Karen's death. Running on this particular day had become for him more of a ritual than an enjoyable outing. A ritual, and a kind of penance; because he knew that memories of that awful train of events would always come flooding back. . . his *indiscretion* with one of his sixth-formers (the euphemism had come from the chairman of governors: King Edward's was a former grammar school, with long-standing traditions and 'standards'). . .his pre-emptive resignation. . . his separation and subsequent divorce from wife, Sheila (who had seethed with righteous indignation when the truth came out, even though their marriage had been rocky for years). . . the note he had received from Karen. . . the shock at reading that she was pregnant. . . and then, before he had managed to respond, the final nightmare: learning that she had died following some squalid back-street abortion. It had sent him off the rails for weeks. Only his new job as a climbing guide – only his beloved mountains – had saved him. But he still thought of Karen. And he still saw her face. Above all, he could still hear the anguished voice of the girl's mother at the inquest, wailing behind her veil. His running and his work had helped in the healing process. They would always help. But he would never be allowed to forget. Never.

There was nothing supernatural in what she was doing. It was all done with bits of glass and the speed of light. Simple as that. Not that it would have seemed simple all those centuries ago when that meddlesome heretic, Galileo, was challenging the orthodoxies of the day. She had read about this recently and it had captured her imagination. If things turned out the way she had planned, she would have good reason to be grateful to the Florentine astronomer. Thanks to his genius she had been able to devise this little deception. Thanks to his pioneering work she now had the power she had been seeking, the power that was exciting her at this moment as she conjured up the creature in her glass. Power: that's what all this was about. The power to foresee, to foreshadow, to foretell – and thus to forearm. She had that now, courtesy of Signor Galileo.

"A-haa. . . " she purred, turning the housing a fraction more, bringing her subject into focus. "Unless someone is wearing his legs…" With deft fingers she made another fine adjustment. "…that's him all right." She was reveling in her superiority, enjoying her advantage. "Yes, that's my boy!"

The definition was excellent. Not only could she identify his legs, she could very nearly read the logo on his shorts.

"Perfect," she sighed, disengaging the eyepiece. "Just perfect."

She slid an affectionate hand along the barrel of the handsome instrument, caressing it almost.

"Yes, I do believe this could be the day. All those years of research. All that tracking, all that planning. Worth every minute now!"

She lowered her head and pressed her lips to the cool casing of her astronomical telescope.

"Thank you, my fine friend," she said. Her lingering kiss, and her breathy words, had caused the shiny brass surface to mist over. "That will be all for today. You can leave it to me now."

Raising her head, she looked out from her lofty vantage point in the window of the attic.

"Come," she cooed, beckoning the moving figure with a theatrical gesture of her right hand. "Come to Mamma!"

With the naked eye, the figure was little more than a dot as yet. But it was slowly getting bigger. Slowly, stride-by-stride, he was moving towards her. Slowly, she was winding him in.

115

"Yes, come into my parlour," she coaxed. Her left hand had released the veil of black lace she had been nervously fingering and was now clasping the handle of a large kitchen knife. "Yes, yes: come on, come in, come up – come-uppance!" she cried. Then she repeated it in a mechanical, staccato voice, as if she were conjugating a Latin verb. "Come on, come in, come up, come-uppance; come on, come in, come up, come-uppance," she cackled, conducting her performance with strong, slashing movements of her knife.

She turned to look at herself in a mirror on the wall. There was a wildness in her eyes, but it did not alarm her. It was born of excitement. She permitted herself a little smile. A controlled smile, but one of triumph. Then she was gone. Suddenly. Out of sight. Down her ladders. Scurrying, like a spider. Gone to set things in motion. She had thirteen minutes in which to do it. This she knew from her research. Thirteen was a magical number, she reflected. But unlucky for some! She herself wasn't superstitious. She believed that sometimes you have to make your own luck. The top two buttons on her blouse had already been undone; now she hitched her skirt a couple inches higher. "That should do it," she said quietly to herself. She knew her man.

He looked ahead, screwing up his eyes for better acuity. Yes, he was sure now that someone was standing outside the farmhouse. And he knew it was her, even from this distance. It was that way she had, without warning, of materializing mysteriously from her surroundings. Today, she had suddenly moved into focus from among the roses that grew along the east side of the building.

He was pleased to see her. For some vague reason, not quite identified – curiosity, perhaps: *there was something about her. . .* – he was always pleased to see her. He had never spoken to her – had never even seen her in close-up: she had a habit of disappearing just as mysteriously as she came into view – but in the last few weeks he had grown accustomed to seeing her about the place. Lately, if for some reason she failed to appear, he had begun to feel disappointed, let down — cheated, even. For, in some strange way, he felt he knew her. It was weird. They had never met; she had only recently moved into the old farmhouse. All he had was a long-shot picture of someone. Someone about his own age. Someone mature, therefore. Mature — but attractive, he fantasized. And perhaps, rather dangerous? Yes, he felt that quite strongly. It was probably why he felt drawn to her. He was a man who liked danger. He had courted it all his life — in the mountains, and in his social life. He sensed danger, yet he felt that he and this woman were destined to meet. Perhaps today would be the day?

Certainly, as he ran along the ancient green lane towards her, things were looking promising. At first she remained stationary. (Observing him, perhaps? He liked to think so. He liked to think that she was taking as much interest in him as he was in her.) Then, as he came closer, she could be seen walking round to the side gate, carrying something. Something heavy, that pulled her right arm straight down, causing her to lean to the left to compensate. She stopped at the gate and set down her burden. Bending over it, she began to busy herself with some task. She was just a yard or two from the grassy path, from the stile he would have to climb in another fifty or sixty strides. Surely their meeting was now inevitable?

"Morning," he sang out as he approached. He saw that she was painting, loading her brush from a large can, trade size. "Grand day."

"Oh," she cried, turning from her task, her free hand flying dramatically to her chest, "you frightened me to death!" Then she laughed nervously. "I'm sorry, I had no idea. Didn't hear you coming. In a world of my own, as usual."

He smiled, inwardly. What was she playing at? Pretending surprise, like that! She must have heard him approach? Yes, of course she had. He was intrigued by her artfulness.

"No, no," he protested, returning her smile. "My fault, coming up on you suddenly like that. Often happens. Don't have a bell, you see."

117

He laughed at his little joke. "Sorry I startled you. Hope I haven't put you off your stroke?"

"Oh, this?" she said, reapplying a forgotten brush to the woodwork, too late to prevent a large blob of paint from splattering her shoe. "I'm just slapping it on. Hardly fine art, is it? Not a lot to spoil, really – except your clothes." She had noticed the paint on her shoe. "Damn! Excuse me a second. I'll have to get this off before it dries."

She kicked off the shoe and bent to pick it up, standing on one leg as she stooped. She almost overbalanced.

"Here," he offered, "let me hold your brush. You're about to run out of hands!"

"Thanks," she said, handing over the brush and pulling out a cloth from the pocket of her skirt. "I'm most awfully sorry about this. I'm delaying you."

She rested her bare foot on the second bar of the gate while she dabbed at the shoe.

"Not at all," he grinned. "It's my pleasure." The shapeliness of her leg had not escaped his notice. Nor had the swell of her breasts, seen through the gap in her low-cut blouse. "My name's Steve, by the way. Steve Merrick. Pleased to meet you."

"I'm Bridget," she said. She left her shoe-cleaning and held out her hand. It felt warm in his. Warm and soft, like a small bird. "Bridget Peters," she smiled. "And I'm pleased to meet you. I don't get many visitors, living alone out here. Sounds sad, perhaps," she purred, her broad smile puckering the skin around her twinkling eyes, "but you've probably made my day." Now she laughed – teasingly, as if at the improbability of this notion. The laughter shook her bosom slightly.

He was suddenly aware that he still had hold of her hand. Smiling apologetically he relaxed his grip, but she seemed reluctant to withdraw. The fractional delay created a moment of intimacy that both delighted and surprised him. She seemed perfectly relaxed, this woman. Almost as if she knew him. He felt an odd flicker of danger

118

again. Just a frisson. It quickly passed as he looked into her eyes. He was captivated. She had such an alluring smile. A rather flirty, mischievous sort of smile. It vaguely reminded him of someone.

No matter. His luck was in. *A smile and a body to die for!*

FLY FISHING

"Stay back!" the man cried, twisting his body to snarl at the approaching figure.

The vehemence of his warning caused him to teeter alarmingly on the low wall, and for one awful moment it looked as if he would lose his balance and fall the ninety feet to the road below.

"Okay, okay!" responded the new arrival, slowing down and raising his palms in a show of innocent neutrality. "Take it easy, okay?"

"Take it easy? Christ, you don't know how bloody stupid that sounds! Never mind take it easy, you just stay back – right?"

The repeated warning was delivered in a voice that still croaked with anguish, but the new arrival was relieved to see that the man had regained his balance. He still looked panicked, but at least he was no longer swaying in such an alarming manner.

"You deaf, or something?" he added quickly. "Not a step further, understand? Or I'll go now."

He was wearing a thick, white polo-neck sweater, the sort seamen wore during the Second World War, and he began to smooth it down over his hips, as if tidying himself up to meet someone. It seemed an odd gesture. But the mode of dress itself was strange, surely? Incongruous, somehow. He might have been on the prom somewhere, standing on a low sea wall, pulling his jumper down for protection against an on-shore breeze. Except up there, high above the traffic and the throng of ant-sized pedestrians, the air was warm and still.

"That's better. Now, you stay right there – or I warn you, I'm off!"

"Of course, mate. Anything you say. Just relax, okay?"

The new arrival had finally halted his advance and had lowered himself into a sitting position on the wall some twenty yards away.

"That's it," he soothed. "Nice and easy. No cause for panic. I'm not the police. Nor the fire brigade. Nobody like that. So why not step down? Or at least step back a bit. You're making me feel nervous."

"Who are you, then?" the man enquired, making some concession by moving his feet to take a wider stance. He had on a pair of white jogging trainers, and as he moved, one of the small reflector strips caught the light. Thankfully, he sounded a little calmer now.

"Just a bloke, that's all. An ordinary bloke off the street. The name's Harry. And yours?"

"Mind your own bloody business!" The snarl had returned. There was a pause during which he gave Harry a hard stare. "Seems dodgy to me, you turning up like this. Out of nowhere. What the fuck are you doing up here if you're just an ordinary bloke?"

"Yes, it must seem odd, I suppose," Harry said, trying to appear calm and relaxed. "I was just passing, that's all, and I happened to look up. Must've caught a movement. And there you were. In some sort of danger, I thought."

"Well, you thought fucking wrong!" the man snapped. "Danger? No, I'm leaving all that behind. All I have to do. . ." and the man moved closer to the edge "is step off. Not dangerous. Not difficult. Easy. A child could do it."

"Of course — but what of the consequences? What happens afterwards?"

"Who'll care? I won't! Anyway, my choice. No concern of yours," the man snapped. Looking across at Harry, he paused for a moment. "Don't tell me you're one of them bloody do-gooders?"

"No, I've told you," Harry insisted. "I'm just a bloke off the street. Someone just passing. But I thought. . ."

"Just passing, were you? Well, Harry Samaritan, whoever you are, you're wasting your bloody time with me. My mind's made up. So why don't you just piss off back down there and, like a good little Levite, pass by on the other side." He had suddenly become excitable again.

"Or. . ." and his mouth twisted into an odd little smile "go and help some little old lady across the road, why don't you – though she probably wouldn't thank you for your trouble, either. Anything – but leave me alone. Just mind your own fucking business!"

"But I couldn't just stand there and do nothing while you - you know?"

"Do myself in? Kill myself?" The man laughed. "Why don't you come out with it? No big deal. I'd have done it by now if you hadn't interrupted me." He paused to swallow his obvious annoyance. "Why did you have to come up here, eh? I mean, would you want some total stranger meddling in your life, telling you when and how to end it? I'll bet you would! No, just leave me, please." His voice sounded weary now. "Leave a bloke to end it in peace."

"In pieces, you mean!" Harry forced a laugh. "Have you any idea how fast you'll fall? And what'll happen when you hit the ground from this height? Not pretty, I can tell you. And – this is the worst bit – you could survive!" He paused to study the man's face. "That's right: you may not even kill yourself. You might actually survive. Then what? Fancy a lifetime in a wheelchair, do you? Or being permanently plugged into some hideous machine, with only its bleeps for company? It's rare, survival from this height. But it has been known. Miracles do happen."

"Miracle talk, eh?" said the man contemptuously. "I reckon I was right about you. One of the God-squad, aren't you? I thought so. That's all I need – a Jesus freak! Well, piss off! My soul's not on offer."

"You couldn't be more wrong about me," laughed Harry. "But what about you? A man who knows the Bible, but seems to be in denial. There's a puzzle."

"Think so, do you? Well, sorry to disappoint you, but there's no mystery. I often used to read the Bible. A lot of atheists do. Know your adversary: that's my motto. Argue from a position of strength."

"Ah, I'm dealing with a rationalist, am I?" Harry cried. "So a rational man takes his own life, does he?"

"He does if he finds his life too painful to bear. If he has no wife, no job, no house, no prospects — no fucking hope! How's that for rational stock-taking?" The man closed his eyes. His anguish was etched on his face. "Can't see a way out, you see. No way of going on. No reason for living. Pain too great. Simple as that."

"But you could get a job. Intelligent man like you. Not old. And educated — yes? You shouldn't have any trouble. Then a job could quickly lead to a house — or some sort of roof over your head. You must know that; you're not stupid."

"Don't you patronize me!" the man cried, coming over all jumpy again. "You're telling me nothing I haven't told myself."

"Well then?"

"Well then — what?"

Perhaps it was merely Harry's perception — but hadn't the man moved closer to the edge again?

"You can talk about jobs and houses," the man went on. "That's the easy bit. But what about wives? Can you find me another wife? And not just any wife. Can you give me back my wife?"

Just for a moment, Harry looked uncomfortable. What did the man mean? What was he asking?

"Or at least," the man continued, "Can you find me another woman I could love — could worship, indeed — the way I loved my wife. The way I thought she loved me." He paused. "You can't, can you? You know you can't."

"Well, I can't guarantee it, of course. But there must be hundreds, thousands, of women out there who would — "

"What? Fit the bill? Meet the job description?" He tossed his head in contemptuous laughter. "Yes, thousands — but none like the woman I've lost. No, it's no good." He stepped forward again; his feet were now perilously close to the edge. "You're wasting your time."

"She died, then, your wife?" enquired Harry, trying desperately to buy time, and trying to sound genuinely interested.

"Died!" cried the man, almost in tears. "Did she buggery! She was taken from me. Stolen. By some unfeeling bastard!" He was really agitated now, throwing his arms about, shifting his feet, swaying alarmingly. Harry was seriously worried: he could take off any second! "And if there's any justice in this life, he'll get his come-uppance."

"Bit harsh, that, don't you think?" responded Harry. "A bit simplistic, surely? I mean to say, it takes two to tango remember. Your wife must've played her part – yes? People don't do things against their will. Not in this day and age."

"Don't they?"

The man closed his eyes; he seemed to be reconsidering the question. There was a long pause. A frightening pause. He was very close to the edge. Harry was worried that without visual cues to rely on, he could well become disorientated and topple forwards. Over the edge. Into oblivion. Thankfully, the man opened his eyes again.

"No, perhaps you're right." he said. "It is possible, I concede, that a woman may not be entirely innocent. Yes. . ." and his eyes closed a second time. "It's not easy to accept that this might apply to my wife, but I am aware that women do have their little ways, that they can beguile."

"Good!" cried Harry, shuffling his seated body along the wall. "That's better. Now you're talking. You're starting to question." He smiled. "Starting to rationalize. Yes, that's more like it. Time to forget – to forgive, even? Time to move on?" There being no protest from the man, Harry was encouraged to continue – and as he did so, he moved a little closer. "Yes, get out there. Instead of feeling sorry for yourself, put yourself about. Plenty of fish left in the sea. Attractive, eager fish. Fish just waiting to be caught. What d'you say?"

"You could be right. If only I could bring myself. . ."

The man looked utterly worn out. His voice sounded tired, defeated. Alarmingly, he seemed to be drifting off – something you can't afford to do when you are standing on a narrow wall ninety feet above the ground. Was he really having second thoughts, Harry wondered? Perhaps a new strategy was called for?

"Know what I think?" Harry said, breaking the silence as he moved along the wall another yard or so.

"No," replied the man, opening his eyes. If he had noticed that Harry was now only three or four yards away, he didn't show it. He looked dejected. "But I have a feeling," he said in a resigned voice, "that you're going to tell me."

"Well, I don't think you're going to jump," said Harry. "In fact, I don't think you ever intended to jump." He waited for the man to protest, becoming worried that he might have misjudged the situation, that he might have blown it. But there was no denial; just the man's vacant stare. "No, I think you're bluffing!" he dared to venture. "I think like most suicide attempts – if we can call this an attempt – that this is simply a cry for help. Am I right?"

"Ah, the evangelist turned psychologist," drawled the man wearily. "Think you've cracked it, do you? Go on."

"Well," said Harry, "who wears a white sweater if they don't want to draw attention to themselves? What better way to catch the eye of someone down there than to dress in white? And with flashing trainers, for good measure!"

He paused for a response, but the man merely fixed him with an unblinking stare.

"Plus," continued Harry, emboldened, "I think this isn't the first time you've been up here. I think it was you I saw this time last week. I saw someone, certainly. Someone in white, too. Caught a glimpse from my office window." Harry pointed. "The block opposite. Tenth floor. I always work late on Thursdays – and as I was closing the

125

window, I definitely saw someone. That's probably why I looked up today. I'm right aren't I? It was you – yes?"

The man didn't answer. He simply turned round, lowered himself into a sitting position, put his head in his hands and began to sob.

Sighing with relief, Harry felt it was now safe to move to a position alongside his forlorn companion, and for several minutes the two men sat together, their legs dangling, their backs to the fearful drop behind them, the silence broken only by occasional sniffs and snuffles. Harry's heart went out to the man. This could be anybody, he thought. Anyone could find himself in this desperate situation.

Suddenly, from a distance but getting closer, Harry could hear the distinctive sound of sirens. The rescue services, perhaps? He turned his trunk to look down into the street. A small knot of people had gathered. Their concerned voices drifted up to him.

He returned his attention to his pitiable companion. The man was calmer now, but Harry could see threads of saliva hanging from his chin. He put his left arm round the man's shoulder and reached for his handkerchief with his free hand.

"Here," he said tenderly, "clean up, eh? Then let's go down, shall we? You know – save them the trouble. Before they start setting things up. We don't need them, do we?"

"No," said the man meekly. Then his voice changed. "Well, I don't anyway." And with that, he swung his right arm violently across Harry's chest and toppled him backwards into the abyss. Then, without looking behind him, he walked towards the door to the rooftop.

"You were right, Harry Sampson," he laughed, "there are plenty of fish out there. But only one very big fish. Only one very special fish. And all I had to do, Harry-Wife-Stealer, was make sure I used the right bait!"

Two minutes later, he met a red-faced policeman as he was descending the staircase.

126

"I'm so sorry," he said, his tear-stained face etched with the agony of his ordeal. "Did what I could. Got him talking. Thought I had him at one stage. But then he suddenly broke free and. . ." He put his hand over his face and began to sob. "Oh, too awful!" he cried, his voice thick with mucus. "The poor, poor man."

FINDING A PIECE OF SKY

He sat on the grass verge looking up at the sky. His knees were bent to a right angle and his inclined trunk was supported by straight arms locked at the elbow. Viewed from the side, he had decided, he might look like a big M. Or better still, an upside-down W. He was glad he had formed a shape and given it a name. Now he could relax and look at the clouds.

He loved clouds. They were his friends. Friends he had studied from pictures in his *Cloud Atlas*, a big book full of photographs that he had purchased for himself from his gardening money. The book was in his 'going away' bag if he needed it. For the moment, he simply wanted to gaze up at them and admire. He was a big cloud gazer. A cloud dreamer, quite often. He had long since learned to recognize them, of course. He could match what he saw in the sky with what he remembered from the atlas. Cloud spotting, he called it.

What he really loved was the shape of the clouds, the restless, changing form of them. For they were never still, even when they appeared to be stationary. Not when you concentrated, they weren't – which was what he was doing now. And not when you looked *into* them rather than *at* them, they weren't – which, again, was what he was doing now, imagining himself a part of them, a tiny particle of ice or water surrounded by millions of brother-particles. You were never alone with clouds. He loved, too, the shape of the sky between them when two or more clouds were sailing close together. It was fun predicting how long it would take for that changing piece of blue to become totally absorbed as the welcoming fingers of one cloud reached out to receive those of another.

"Want a lift, mate?" The driver was big and square and solid, like his lorry. "Well, do you – yes or no?" His face was round, like a full moon, and his smile pushed his cheeks up into little apple shapes. It was a face the boy felt he could trust. He got awkwardly to his feet and reached for his bag. He knew he was making a tall, thin shape now. *Like a bean-pole*, Aunt Ellie had once said. Except he stooped from the shoulders, so he liked to think of himself as more like a sunflower. "Better climb up, then. Mind your head."

The inside of the cab was very interesting. The instrument panel, particularly. There were lots of shapes. Circles and squares and triangles, mainly. All very familiar in themselves, but it was the way they were arranged, and the shapes between them, that caught his attention. He quickly clocked and registered the lay-out of the panel, then settled back in his seat and looked ahead through the wide rectangle of glass in front of him. It was like a huge TV screen upon which, as the lorry picked up speed, he could see not only the road opening up before him, but also a large expanse of cloud-studded sky. He spent some time taking in the shapes of roadside signs, buildings, vehicles, trees and bushes; but pretty soon it was the broad skyscape that absorbed him.

The windscreen was really a much bigger version of the viewfinder he often made with his fingers. It formed a frame around the sky – and this morning the sky was very busy. It teemed with fluffy, white, cotton-wool clouds of different shapes and sizes. Most of them moved slowly in small schools – for safety, he imagined – but one or two bold ones had ventured forth alone. *Cumulus*, they were called. He was drawn to that word, *cumulus,* when he found it in his book. He liked its individual letters – all but one of them so curved and soft, like the cloud itself – and he loved the shape they made when they were put together. He even liked the long, thin letter 'l', the odd one out, appreciating it for being the slender thread by which the cloud hung from the roof of the sky.

"Going far?" asked the lorry driver, keeping his eyes on the road. There was no reply. His youthful passenger was lost in the clouds. "I see," the driver smiled. "Cat got your tongue?"

"Don't have a cat. Don't like cats."

"Ah," said the driver, "what do you like, then?"

"I like Aunt Ellie. I like clouds. They're my friends. I like shapes. And I like jigsaws."

"Jigsaws, eh? I'm not so fond, myself. Can never seem to finish the buggers. But you're probably good at them. Anyway, what's your name, young man? Mine's Fred."

"I like oxtail soup, as well," returned the youth. "Better than tomato."

"Ah, I see: we're back on likes, are we?" smiled the driver. "Well, I have to say I'm with you all the way when it comes to oxtail. But what do they call you? As I said, I'm Fred."

"Robinson."

"No – Small. My name's Fred Small. And yours?"

"Robinson."

"Oh, I see, *your* name's Robinson?" The driver grinned. "Sorry, I'm being stupid. So what's your first name, then?"

"Robinson. I told you."

"Ah, got you! As in Robinson Crusoe, you mean?"

"No. My name's Robinson Wyke."

"Yes, well, pleased to meet you, Robinson Wyke." The driver took one hand off the wheel and touched his forehead in a little salute. His hands, the youth noticed, were big and square, with black, bristly hair sprouting below the knuckles. "So, where're you going? Where do you want dropping?"

"'Don't know," said the youth, his voice trailing off; his head was back in the clouds.

"Don't know? Not sure I know where that is!" The driver chuckled at his little joke, but there was puzzlement knitted into his brow.

"Okay – but when you decide, you will give me plenty of notice, won't you? You know – big wagon like this. . . dangerous otherwise." There was no reply. The driver didn't persist.

Robinson particularly liked *cumulo-nimbus*. It had twelve letters, twelve pieces, that you could pile one on top of another to make a huge tower. This was fitting, he thought, because he knew that cumulo-nimbus is the tallest of all the clouds, sometimes towering up to a height of fifty thousand feet. The biggest. The highest. That's why it was called *Cloud Nine*. Not many people knew that. Even a name like *stratus*, though, had taken his fancy. True, it didn't appear spectacular like cumulo-nimbus; but it was interesting to him because its shape – all pieces low, forming an even layer – seemed to match the type of cloud it described. He knew all words by their shape rather than by their sound. He was really more of a word-spotter than a reader, and cloud-words were his favourites. He kept them in his head. Pictures were his friends. He never tried to speak them. Making them, though, and remembering them: that was fun. It was enough. Trying to make sounds from his pictures often tripped him up. And it hurt when people laughed.

"Have you decided yet?"

"Sorry."

"Ah, off again, were you?" The driver's smile remained good-natured, indulgent. "I was just saying, have you decided yet? You know. Where you're going. Where you want me to drop you."

"Not sure," Robinson said, sleepily. He had been dreaming up a story from the cloud-pictures on his screen. "To find a shape. To smell the sea. To hear the cry of gulls. That's where I'm going."

"Eh?" laughed the driver. Robinson didn't respond. He was looking at the clouds again. "I see," the driver attempted, "somewhere by the sea, you think? Yes. good clue, that. Hundreds of miles of coastline –

131

should be a doddle!" He shook with laughter. "You might have to do a bit better than that, lad. Is there nothing else you can tell me? You know, to give me a bit more of a clue, like?"

"Sorry?"

"I was just wondering if you could be a bit more helpful. You know – anything else? To help us pin it down it a bit?"

"Not really. Only," Robinson closed his eyes. "I think *he* might have lived there."

"He? Who's he?"

"You know – that man. Him with the merry men."

"Ah, Robin Hood, you mean? No, he lived in Sherwood Forest. Down Nottingham way. Miles from the sea, that is!" The driver scratched at his untidy thatch of black hair. "Not sure I can help you. I'm going past Scarborough, if that's any help. That's by the sea."

"Don't know. Not sure. Just drop me anywhere. I'll find it. One day I'll find it. I know I will."

"Well, the best of luck, my friend. Wish I could help in your search, but I've got to press on. I'm new to this run, and I've got to be in Hull by lunchtime. So if you don't mind I'll find somewhere safe to pull up. That be all right? Sorry, I'd like to be more. . . hey, what about this sign coming up. See it? *Robin Hood's Bay*! Might that be it?"

"Don't know. Can't say." Robinson looked downcast. "I can't smell the sea." Then he brightened a little. "But Robin Hood, you say?"

The driver put him down right underneath the road sign, and Robinson spent a few moments examining the size and shape of the words and their constituent letters. Once he had registered them, he shouldered his bag and set off down a steep hill. Round the first bend the road got even steeper. Round the second bend it became steeper still. It was alarming. He had never met a road as steep as this one. It was all he could do to stay on his feet.

He feared what it might be like round the next bend, but what awaited him caused his heart and his spirits to lift. For there, far below him, he could see the sea, sparkling like a jewel in the morning sunlight. He stood for several minutes simply staring at the view, taking in the sea and the sky above it, trying to determine where the one met the other, marvelling at the colours, and at the shapes of the clouds. Then he set off again, sniffing the air as he walked. Yes, yes – he was sure he could smell the sea!

When he came alongside the village sign, he stopped and scratched his head. It was done in different lettering – big, bold, capital lettering that slightly altered the shapes of the words – and it threw him for a couple of minutes. But they could only say *Robin Hood's Bay*, he decided; so although he was still not certain that this was the place he was looking for, he recorded a mental picture of the new word-shapes and continued his descent.

He could now see, a short way ahead of him, three or four tall, pillar-shaped houses standing back from the line of the cliffs. As he approached, he noted the shapes of their windows, doors, roofs, gable-ends, chimney stacks and pots. He also took in the shape of a gathering of large birds perched on one of the roof ridges. Just as he came alongside, a car back-fired – and suddenly, almost as one, the birds took off, filling the air with a din of flapping wings and shrill, protesting squawks. Ah, first the smell of the sea, and now the sound of gulls! Was this the place he was looking for? Was this where he would find *The Shape*, the shape so clearly fixed inside his head, the shape he had carried with him for over thirteen years? Ever since he was four, according to Aunt Ellie. And for almost as long as he could remember, he had promised himself that one day he would go off in search of his shape. One day he would find it; one day he would find out. He had told no one of this. Not even Aunt Ellie. Not even Mr Jones, who had given him his gardening job. And now, at last, here he was; on the verge of discovery. Hopefully, somewhere down there –

down in that jumble of buildings thrown higgledy-piggledy together – was the shape he was looking for.

He was very excited. It was like doing his jigsaws. The sorting; the thrill of the search – and that special moment when he would find a key piece, a piece that would help him make sense of a whole section. How clumsy his fingers would feel as he tried nervously to fit it into place! Oh, if only he could find *this* piece, see where it belonged, see how it fitted, it would help him complete his own picture.

He passed a road going off to his right. To where, he had no idea. The word-shape on the sign was very interesting, but it was foreign to him. The road he was on now dropped straight down to the sea. It was very steep, and too narrow in places to take more than one vehicle. And there were people everywhere. He didn't know it, but the incoming tide was starting to drive them from the beach. In their dozens, they funneled into the road. It was the only place for them to go. Apart from the shops and the pubs, of course: they were doing a roaring trade.

As he descended, the road became more and more crowded. Robinson didn't like crowds. In fact, apart from Aunt Ellie (who wasn't a real aunt, but he loved her) and Mr. Jones (kind Mr. Jones, who let him work in his garden after he left his special school) he didn't like people very much at all. They were noisy; they asked too many questions – and they laughed at you when you were day-dreaming, or when you got things wrong. He preferred to be alone, to live quietly inside his head. He didn't like to have his peace disturbed. So it was with great relief that he was able to avoid the noisy knot of people toiling up the hill towards him by turning off to his right.

He found himself in a ginnel so narrow that a person reaching out from the window of one house could almost shake hands with a person in the house opposite. There were scores of alleyways like this one. Forming a network of pathways between the tightly packed houses on both sides of the road, they were a characteristic feature of the village. Those to the west – the ones Robinson found himself exploring to begin with – ended in cul-de-sacs high up on the side of the moor; those to the east, after much tortuous twisting and turning, terminated in tiny yards, the size of pocket handkerchiefs, perched precariously on the cliff top.

The houses were tall and thin. They had to be to get so many to stand together, cheek-by-jowl, like that. They reminded him of the plants in Mr. Jones' garden: how they grew up and up, tall and straight, competing for the light. He was delighted by the way the buildings came and left the ginnels at different angles, by their many roof levels, by the number and variety of their chimney pots, and by the small size of some of the windows and doors. So much to see. So much variation. It was fascinating, all of it – but it was not quite what he was looking for. He took it all in, yes – but his eyes were mainly focused on the spaces between the houses, just as they were focused so often on the spaces between his precious clouds. In every ginnel his head was inclined, his eyes looking upwards. He knew what he was looking for. If it should be here, he would find it. He knew he would. This place was perfect, full of promise. But he was tiring. Everywhere was so steep. So many steps. Up and down, up and down, up and down, all through the morning and into the afternoon. And as fatigue set in, he had to be careful. The pathways were so uneven, and there were so many steps. He tended to be somewhat clumsy at the best of times, so it was hardly surprising that on several occasions he nearly lost his footing. He had to take a break.

With the labyrinth of ginnels to the west fully explored, he walked down the road and sat on the sea wall to eat his lunch. There were two loaves of bread and two tins of oxtail soup in his bag – and he had remembered the tin opener! He had been planning this trip for some time. He had come prepared. He would not go hungry. Bread dunked in oxtail soup – delicious, even if the soup was cold! And there were apples to follow, and a big bottle of Tizer to wash it all down with. He liked Tizer. He suddenly thought: he should have mentioned that in the list he had given to Fred, the lorry driver.

His little feast had perked him up again. Now he couldn't wait to get started on the maze of alleyways leading up to the top of the cliff. He had spied the houses while he was dunking his bread, marvelling at the way they clung together on the steep ground. Take one away and the whole pack would fall down! The thought had amused him. He was still chuckling when he entered the first ginnel.

If anything, the houses on this side of the road were even closer together. That gave him hope. Time and time again, as he ascended, he would turn a corner and be presented suddenly with a new shape – a shape made not only by the building features themselves, but by a piece of sky between them; or, as he neared the edge of the cliff, by a piece of the sea. He was almost dizzy with excitement. Every narrow alleyway, every house along the way, was like a new jigsaw box being opened for him, its pieces, all new and bright and sharp-edged, spread out in front of him, ready to be sorted, ready to be memorized, ready to be assembled.

But as the afternoon wore on, Robinson's excitement began to evaporate. What he had seen was new and vivid and memorable, but he had not found what he was looking for. And once again, fatigue was slowing him down. In truth, it often did. "Just outgrown his strength, that's all. Not lazy." That had been Mr. Jones' generous verdict on his new lanky gardener, having found him resting in the strawberry patch on his first day. And he was right. Robinson got through each day by resting between great bursts of energy. Like a small child. And now the child was flagging fast.

His hopes were flagging, too. From a small yard on the cliff edge, where one of the ginnels had terminated, he had been able to assess what was left for him to explore. Two or three alleyways, that was all – before he would reach the wide gap separating the old part of the village from the newer houses above. He had a feeling – though he

136

wasn't sure why – that the newer part of the village to the north would not be as promising.

The next ginnel was so narrow, with so many tight twists and elbow turns – not to mention steps and pavements that were uneven and crumbling in places – that he reached the top of it feeling that he had spent too much time looking down at his feet. As he made his way down again, just to be sure, he kept screwing his neck round to look back along the alleyway. On one occasion he twisted his trunk round as well, an action which came at an unfortunate moment, just as the next step down, lower than expected, upset his balance.

Down, down – seven or eight steps down – he tumbled, his body folding at one stage to send his legs flying over his head. During this movement, his bag – which had initially given him some protection – fell from his shoulder and hit the pavement with a loud bang as the fizzy Tizer bottle exploded. He came to rest where the ginnel jinked sharply to the right. His body had crashed into a closed doorway with such force that his head was thrown back to knock thunderously on the solid, wooden door. At that point, he lost consciousness.

He came round to find himself still lying in the doorway, but the door was now open. His head lay across the threshold, supported by a cushion; his wet bag lay on the ground beside him. An elderly woman with a cloud of white hair was smiling down at him.

"It's all right, lad, I think you'll live. No bones broken, I reckon. Just a bit blood, that's all. Soon have that sponged off. Looks worse than it is. But next time you come a-calling, try tapping on the door with your hand like everyone else!" The cloud above her shook with laughter. "Well, I never did! What a thing to happen."

Robinson didn't respond. He had only just opened his eyes. He was still gathering his wits. Turning his gaze away from the woman, he looked across the corner to where the steps had taken their turn. In his dazed state he thought he saw, between two houses, a piece of sky he had not noticed before. *Was that...?* He closed his eyes, then

137

opened them again. Just to be sure. *Was that it...? Yes, it was!* There before him was *The Shape*. He had found it!

"I said, what a thing to happen to you."

"I'll say! What a thing." And it was Robinson's turn to laugh. He didn't often laugh. Except when he was in his clouds, and with his jigsaws, life was seldom a laughing matter. "Yes, you can say that again. What a thing!"

"Are you sure you're all right, lad? I mean, I wouldn't have thought there was much to laugh at, nearly breaking your neck like that."

"I'm fine." Robinson laughed again. "Over the moon! On Cloud Nine! I've found it, you see."

"Found what?"

"The Shape! I've found where I used to live. I used to play out there, you see. I know I did. And sometimes I'd stop and look up – look up at a gull on the roof, or at a cloud. Yes, I know that space." She followed his eyes up to the long strips of sky between the chimney pots, to a triangle sticking out, where one roof sloped down to meet another, and to a straight, pointy-finger bit where the right-hand wall met the roof. "It's the piece I've been looking for. Yes, I'm sure. I used to live in that house!" He paused to point with a flat hand. "That first one, the one on the left. That's where I lived. I know I did."

The woman didn't seem to share his joy. Not at first, she didn't. She was frowning. She looked mystified.

"No, you can't be," she said, eventually. "Surely not. And yet. . ." She was now staring at him, her eyes searching his features. "What's your name, lad? Do you mind telling me your name?"

"Robinson. My name's Robinson Wyke."

"Oh, my good Lord!" The woman threw her arms into the air. "Well, I never! She turned to shout into the room. "George – you'll never guess who's dropped in to see us. It's Robin's son – God rest his soul. Robin and Martha Wyke's lad. God rest her soul, an' all. And he's recognized the house. Don't ask how. God moves in mysterious ways.

Any road, he's recognized it. Glory be – he's come home! Robinson's come home."

"I'm right then, am I?"

"I'll say. George and me knew your mam and dad well. In fact, we nearly took you in ourselves. You know – after the. . ." She paused and sucked in her breath. "Such a shame! But there, you've made a fine young man. Somebody's been taking good care of you. Them and the Good Lord, I should say. And all's well that ends well, as they say."

The woman helped him into the house. The room was low and small, and rather gloomy. Except under the window. There he noticed straightaway a large, square table. And on that table was a picture.

"You do jigsaws?" Robinson's face lit up.

"Yes – it's a bit of a, what-do-you-call-it? An obsession, I'm afraid. Done 'em all my life. In fact, young as you were, you used to drop in sometimes and do one with me. Well, if the truth be known, you used to help me out. You were very good. Some really difficult ones, you helped me with. You know – them that's all flowers, or all sea. Diabolical, they are, some of them!'

She was still looking at him full in the face, but her eyes were no longer examining. They had a misty, far-away look. For a few moments she seemed lost in another world. Then suddenly her eyes were dancing again.

"Well, what are you waiting for, lad? Draw up a chair. You're obviously very good at finding bits of sky."

A CHANGE IN THE LANDSCAPE

"Nothing changes, then?"

They were not far now from the cliff-top path. Scabious had appeared in the field verges. They could smell the sea. This could be the last stile.

"Really?" She waved him forward. "No, please – you go first." She laughed. "I might need a hand down."

"You and me both," he grinned, going ahead, stepping up somewhat unsteadily. "Good job I've got my stick."

He took her hand and received the unbalanced weight of her as she stepped down.

"Sorry – my hands are sticky," she said, wiping them quickly on the back of her crops. "No, they are! I'm sweating like a pig."

"Horse, surely," he smiled, falling in behind her, happy to watch the movement of her bottom. "Isn't that how it goes? Horses sweat, men perspire – and you ladies just glow?"

"Oh, we glow all right – but mainly when we're sweating!" She stopped and turned to face him with that familiar grin. "And ladies of a certain vintage do an awful lot of glowing. But what never changes?" She was amused. Their conversations were often disjointed like this. "You mean, this walk?" She closed her eyes and threw open her arms, as if to embrace the landscape. "You mean, all this?"

"Oh, just musing aloud, I think." He loved that grin. They had laughed about it all those years ago. *Like the cat who's had the cream,* he used to say. *Or the Cheshire Cat in Alice,* she would respond – and they would giggle, in those far-off days, at the thought of someone slowly vanishing, leaving only their smile behind. He grinned back. "Don't mind me."

It wasn't the last stile as it turned out; there were two more. Two

140

more chances to notice the swing of her bosom as he caught her weight in handing her down. And two more full-frontal grins.

Their narrow path was running straight for the sea along one side of adjacent fields of barley. *Same path – same fields, surely – from all those years ago? And it was always barley.* Today, the corn was waist high and heavy-eared, almost ready for harvesting. For the moment, though, it was a sea of old gold rocked into gentle waves by the light breeze.

The final stile brought them down onto a path running north-south along the line of the mudstone cliffs; in places, it ran perilously close to the edge. *Closer than the old days, surely?*

They turned north, heading for Eyehope Dene. Lining the path to the left there were tall, bearded grasses, pale and wistful, like the ghosts of barley. Lesser bindweed threaded its way between the stalks, and closer to the ground there were patches of vetch and stunted cranesbill. The plant life was all much as they remembered it from thirty years ago when they were biology students from the university, escaping the city.

It was warm work. They began looking ahead for a suitable picnic spot. After a few minutes they dropped down into a small hollow scooped out of the eroding cliff, now grassed over. It looked ideal. Soon they were breaking into their sandwiches, amidst coltsfoot and little clusters of sea thrift.

"I meant you," he said suddenly, screwing up the lid on his drink and resting his back against the cushioning vegetation. "You haven't changed."

"Get away!" *That grin again.* "White hair, wrinkles, spongy tummy, dodgy knees – flattering yes, but no marks for observation."

"Perhaps we see what we want to see?" he suggested. "Not important, that ageing stuff. Love makes it irrelevant. No, I meant – you're still dreaming?"

"Of course I am." Her eyes had a misty, far-away look. "I, we, have

141

no choice."

"There is always choice." He took her hand and brought it to his lips.

"But I can't just leave him. That would be unthinkable." She withdrew her hand. "It's not his fault, is it? Please don't go there. That's not like you."

"Perhaps not. But where does it leave us?"

"With a very lovely dream." She leaned across and kissed him lightly on the cheek. "You were all I wanted, you know. All those years ago. Then you were gone. So what else but to dream?" Her moist eyes suddenly brightened. "And then – wow! – just when I'd almost given up, there you were, thanks to 'Facebook', back in my life again. Only this time it's me who's not available."

He laughed. "Crap timing, as usual! But you're quite good at it, aren't you?"

"What?"

"The dreaming."

"Well, I've had enough practice," she grinned.

"True, but it isn't just that," he persisted. "You've had to dream. I get that. And I'm in there with you, sharing the bubble. But whereas I'm always chafing for reality, I get the feeling that you can go on and on and on. Just living the dream."

"Yes, I probably can," she said. "If I have to. But better the dream, would you say, than one of us walking away?"

This was met with silence. And a serious face.

"Hey, come on," she chivvied, "cheer up! We've got today – and what a lovely day it is, too! And we've got each other. Things can change. Who knows what the future might hold?"

"Cut off by the tide might be one thing!" he quipped, looking at his watch. And suddenly he was on his feet and gathering things into the rucksack. "High tide's not till four, but I think we should be making a move. The path into *The Dene* is steep, remember. And then we still

142

have to get round *The Nose*. So look lively, my girl! No more dreaming."

Eyehope Dene was one of many in these parts where the sea had cut back deeply into the cliffs to form steep-sided valleys long since colonized by ash, oak and sycamore, and made almost impenetrable by phalanxes of nettle, bramble and stunted willow. The only way down to the beach was by a series of steps, steep and uneven, cut into the cliff side. This pathway, although used frequently, could be rather overgrown in places, and in wet conditions it could be treacherous.

Today it was mercifully dry, but the going was tough. The woman needed support as she lowered herself from several of the steeper steps, and they were often taken unawares by overhanging branches, clutched at by brambles and, lower down, stung by vindictive nettles. It was therefore with some relief that they reached the floor of the Dene and began to follow the narrow stream – first on one bank, then on the other – that was soon to lose itself in a shelf of pebbles.

As they rested on the beach for a few minutes, perched on ground-down molars of magnesian limestone, they looked south along the beach, trying to gauge the state of the tide.

"I think we can relax," he said. "The water's nowhere near the point."

"Yes, but that can't be *The Nose,* surely? Isn't it too close?" Beneath her gentle questioning, she sounded sure of herself. "And anyway, it's not obvious enough, is it? Should be more prominent. More . . . yes," she laughed. "More like a nose! It must be further round."

"I think maybes, you're right," he said, smiling at his use of the vernacular. "You forget, don't you? Well, I do. Your memory was always better than mine. Anyway – play it safe, shall we, and make tracks?"

They were silent for the next few minutes. The beach hereabouts, heavily shingled, had them teetering from one large pebble to the next. Initially it demanded all their concentration; their faces were set

143

hard. But slowly, as the stones began to thin out, they were able to relax. They could look ahead now, shielding their eyes against the sun reflecting off the sea, straining to catch a glimpse of *The Nose*, still a little concerned about the tide.

The man's thoughts were also on their earlier conversation. *She had managed in her optimistic way to sound almost hopeful*, he mused. *Yet she was offering no* real *hope, was she? Wasn't she, in fact, rather too accepting of their situation? It had left him feeling uneasy. Unlike her, he wasn't sure how long he could live in the dream.*

Concerns about the incoming tide increased as they approached the promontory he had mistaken for *The Nose*. The waves were now breaking ominously close to their feet, and to avoid getting wet they had to make a run for it, rounding the point holding hands and whooping like a couple of kids. Once clear of the water, he caught hold of her and swung her round in dizzy celebration, only to lose his balance in the attempt and fall back into the sand, her body tumbling heavily on top of him. They shared a salty kiss before she broke free, and the pair lay back in the dry, warm sand, chests heaving, eyes blinking against the sun.

"You daft old bugger!" she laughed. "Could have given yourself a heart attack, giving a duzzy to a fat lass like me. Either that, or a rupture!"

"You're not fat," he protested. "Just cuddly. But I get carried away when I'm with you. Always did." He turned his head to face her grin. "Daft, isn't it? You know – how we can forget that we're no longer as young as we used to be?"

"No, it's not daft," she said, levering herself stiffly to her feet. "I think it's lovely." She shook the sand from her clothing. "But if we want to stay dry, we ought to be moving on. The tide, remember."

From this angle *The Nose* looked a formidable obstacle, and they set off with some urgency, worried now that they could be stranded

144

between the two points. However, as they moved round the small bay and gained a different view, they gradually realized that things were not as they at first seemed. Neither of them said anything for a while; they each walked quietly, containing their amazement until they were absolutely sure that what they were seeing was not a mirage created by the heat haze. And then they blurted their excitement and astonishment, almost simultaneously.

"The Nose!" they cried together.

"How amazing is that?" She turned to him, her face flushed and glistening with perspiration and excitement. *"The Nose* – now a sea stack! Are you sure we're not seeing things?"

"Yes, it's weird! They've always been eroding, these cliffs. But this is weird. To think – just thirty years! So much for the immutable landscape."

"And the fear of being trapped by the tide!" She laughed, and he saw the relief in her face. "Because, thank goodness . . . am I right? It looks as if we can sneak round the back. Over that rubble of rocks – yes? How wonderful! We're going to make it. We're going to stay dry!"

Beyond the wondrous sea stack – *Broken Nose,* they had immediately christened it – the going was easy. They took off their shoes, tying the laces together and slinging them over their shoulders, and walked the final mile, hand in warm hand, feet in warm sand, along the narrow strip of beach into Seaton. Minutes later, having toiled up the steep, uneven steps to the cliff-top car park, they were speeding off to the bus station so that she would be in time to catch the 17.14 back to Hartlepool.

It had been another stolen day together. A delightful sentimental journey, marred only by the usual twinge of sadness at their parting. *The parting of two people who should never have separated all those years ago,* he mused. *Two people who should be together now.* Yet, as he made his way back to his car, there was an unexpected lightness in his step. For some reason – he wasn't at all clear why – he was buoyed by a little swell of optimism.

Perhaps it was the thought of telling his daughter (up for the weekend, and always up for sharing his little adventures) the curious story of Seaton cliff and its rather startling nose job?

BY AVENTURE

He was called James McKinnon – always James, never Jim or Jimmy, he said. Her name was Abi Senior – never Abigail, always Abi, she told him.

She was an art teacher, she volunteered, and he somewhat archly described himself as a 'geriatric lay-about'. He wouldn't say what he used to be when he was once 'perhaps half useful', as he put it. He said it was no longer important.

They met on the Hebridean ferry from Leverbugh to Berneray, a passage that wove its tortuous way through a scattering of small, low islands in the Sound of Harris. The journey was picturesque and full of interest – though it occurred to both of them that it might be tricky to navigate in bad weather.

They had got into conversation because they were the only passengers braving it out on the outside deck. Not that conditions were poor: they weren't. It was dry and visibility was excellent; but the wind seemed to be too 'lively' for their fellow travellers. Seemingly, James and Abi were the only ones who had both the all-weather gear and the determination to miss nothing; they shared a need to actually *feel* the experience, and this had bonded them from the beginning. Yet they made an unlikely couple. She saw a broad, snowy moustache and wisps of white hair flying out from beneath his hat and hood; he saw the bloom of youth on her cheeks and felt the energy that fed her softly spoken words and her easy, adroit movements.

"So what brings you to Uist?" she had asked at one point. "Business, or pleasure?"

"Neither," he said. "You might call it a senior gap year."

"Gap year!" Her smile was amused, slightly puzzled. "What sort of gap? From what to what?"

"Not sure," he replied. "From drowning to trying to cling on to something, perhaps."

"Now you really do have to explain that," she laughed.

"No, I don't," he said. "But by aventure, by chance, I always hope to find something. And I usually do. I travel hopefully. Better than arriving, it's said. Brings arrivals of a different type."

She looked at him quizzically, trying to work this one out. That phrase, by aventure, for example – what did that mean? She liked a man who was not obvious, but this one was unusual, intriguing. However, he wasn't going to be drawn any further.

"Hey, look!" he cried, diverting attention. "That's a cormorant, isn't it?" They were close enough to a tiny island not to need binoculars. "Why do they do that, I wonder? Hang out their wings in that way?"

"I think it's a shag," she said, trying not to sound too teacherly. "Cormorants don't have the shaggy crest. And shags do that – peg their wings out, like sheets – because they don't have a preening gland. They can't water-proof their feathers, so they have to dry them out whenever they can."

"Thanks for that," he said, his smile stretching the brush of his moustache across his face. It made her want to laugh. "I like the image, too. Know about birds, do you?"

"A bit. Not a lot. But I'm interested. All of this interests me," she said, throwing out her arms with a kind of child-like delight. It was almost a benediction.

"Ah, so that's why you're here then? To embrace the great outdoors?"

"Sort of, yes. It feeds me. And I always hope it'll feed my art, the creative me." Then she laughed. "Sounds a bit pompous, all that. Let's just enjoy."

This was about all that passed between them before he said he was getting cold, excused himself and went below. A short time later a voice announced that they were coming in to land. She wasn't to know, but he was a foot passenger, whereas she had her car – 'Little Blue' – to go to, down in the bowels of the boat. They went their separate ways, with no chance to say goodbye.

Four days later she crossed the narrow causeway from South Uist to Eriskay – with its arresting sign, *Caution: Otters Crossing* – and was quickly drawn to a deserted beach on which she could stretch her legs and be alone with her thoughts. Except she wasn't alone.

It started out as a smudge on the low-tide line far ahead of her. A piece of driftwood, perhaps? Or a tangle of kelp? But, no: the distance between them was reducing too quickly. It could only be a person, moving in her direction. She felt a little twinge of resentment. Her beach – invaded! As the figure drew closer, she saw that it was barefooted, saw the boots strung around the neck, made out the face above the boots – and saw, incredibly, that it was him: the gap-year man from the ferry.

"Well, hello again!" she said, forgetting all thought of invaded privacy as they came alongside one another. "How strange is this? But it's good to see you again."

"You, too," he smiled. "Not really that strange, though. Small island. Few people. Beautiful beach. Two outdoor types. The lure of history. The romance of Bonnie Prince Charlie." As he smiled, his eyes twinkled. "Almost inevitable, I'd say."

"Yes, attracts the crowds like a magnet, this stretch of sand," she laughed, and he laughed with her. It didn't surprise her that he too had done his homework. "It drew me before I checked the map, before I realized where we are. And it's where it all started, in a way. The Forty-Five Rebellion. Here, where we stand. Imagine!"

Unhooded and less wrapped-up – for the day was dry and sunny, with only a gentle breeze – she could now see that he was older than she had guessed him to be on the ferry. What – late sixties, perhaps? Yes, she noticed the loose skin in his neck; surely no younger? His hair – white and thin, like thistle down, the short wisps dancing about above a craggy, tanned face – confirmed her impression.

"So, are you staying on Eriskay?" he asked.

She looked younger than he remembered. Probably no more than mid-twenties. And very attractive! Not beautiful, he decided — nose rather too large, eyes rather too close together — but lovely liquid brown eyes that were forever examining the world, forever intelligent.

"No," she said. "But not far away. North of Pollachar. Up the coast, near the dunes. Know it?"

"Yes, I walked along the beach there yesterday," he replied. "Little island opposite. Lots of kelp. Lots of birds. Quiet spot."

"Sure is," she nodded. "And you? Where are you staying?"

"In the dunes tonight," he grinned, pointing back along the beach. "I've sussed out a real cosy little hollow for the night, and now I'm off to the pub for a meal — you know, the *Whisky Galore* place? — before I settle down for the night."

"Camp out every night, do you?" she asked. It wouldn't have surprised her.

"No, no," he laughed. "Getting a bit too long in the tooth for that. Done my share, mind. But I like my creature comforts these days. No, I've been staying in the hostel. Should be on Barragh really. That was the plan. But I missed the ferry. Got carried away in the graveyards!" He chuckled when he saw her face. "Lost all track of time. One of them's a Commonwealth cemetery — unexpected, that — but it's the other one that's packed with the clan McKinnon. Fascinating."

"That why you've taken your boots off?" she twinkled. "Don't want to wake your ancestors as you walk past?"

"Ah, you've remembered my name!" he exclaimed. "I like that."

"And have you remembered mine?"

"Of course," he smiled. "Easy — Abi Senior. Abyssinia!"

"Oh, no," she groaned, "I thought I'd left all that behind in primary school." And again, they laughed together. "But won't there be rats?"

"Not with you, sorry — rats?"

"In the dunes."

"Probably," he grinned. "Rats get everywhere. They say you're never more than ten feet from one. But, walking all day, and no shower – they'll take one whiff of me and be off!"

"What about the pub – *The Politician* – won't they have a bed for the night?"

"They might," he said. "But I've got to be careful. Struggling writer and all that; I might not be able to afford it."

"Really?" She looked at him with renewed interest, he thought.

"Yes," he said. "Not quite down to my last dollar; nothing like that. But I'm on a pretty tight budget."

"No, I meant are you really a writer?"

"Yes," he smiled. "Don't get excited – nobody famous. But yes, I am."

"Are you published?"

"People always ask that!" he laughed. "Yes, a few times – but it's no big deal."

"Would be for me," she said, scarcely concealing her admiration. "It's what I want, you see. More than anything. More than my art, even." She paused. This was the first time she had declared her new-found passion to anyone; an explanation was perhaps called for. She liked things to be explained. "Teaching; two or three exhibitions; a few sales – I've achieved quite a bit, I suppose. And I've loved every minute of it. But now I want to write. I know I do. It's not just me being restless. I feel it here, inside me. A strong urge. And ideas are coming. Words are starting to flow, too." She saw his face. "Sorry, I get carried away."

"No, don't apologize. I like the passion, the intensity, the sense of excitement. And it never leaves you. It returns with each new piece – even if it can then get forgotten in the blood, sweat and tears!"

"Look," she said suddenly, "I shall worry about you out there tonight. How about a comfy bed instead? My cottage has a spare room. I'm afraid you'd have to share the bathroom, but it'd be no trouble. Honestly it wouldn't. And I can give you supper. Nothing fancy – lasagne – but you're welcome to share it. Bottle of wine, too. *The Politician*'s fine, but it's not

151

cheap. And yes, you can tell me all about your writing. And then, in the morning, I can run you over to Cracebhaig and make sure you get that ferry."

"Hey, hold your horses!" He looked at her with a look she recognized: the look of her father. "You're very kind, really you are. But now I worry about you. You hardly know anything about me, Abi. I'm just some hobo you've met on a small island. I could be anybody. Runaway axe murderer, bank robber, rapist – anybody! My daughter's probably twice your age, but it would worry me to death if I thought she was acting rashly like this."

"Yes, that's why I know it'll be all right," she smiled. "I'll be safe, I know, sharing my cottage with you."

"I see – because I'm probably old enough to be your grandfather, you mean?"

"No, not because you're an old man," she said, her liquid eyes fixing him seriously, "but because you're a good man. I just know you are. Call it instinct. And anyway," she added, "I don't see you as an old man, either. Just an interesting man. A man who's known a bit of the world, who's knowledgeable and amusing. A man who likes people and knows how to treat them."

"Okay, okay," he cried, throwing his arms up in mock surrender. "I submit to the flattery! I accept your gracious offer. But you still don't know. Remember that. Instinct's not always to be relied upon. And never trust a writer," he added, smiling broadly, "they tell lies for the fun of it."

"Yes, dad," she laughed.

"You're hopeless!" he said, wagging a finger. "There'll be a delay, I'm afraid. Do you mind? Got to double back to my little hollow. My rucksack's stowed there. The rats will be disappointed to see me go, but they'll get over it. I can meet you out on the road. Somewhere near the causeway? In about an hour, say? Sorry to put you out."

He's right, she thought, as she was driving back across the causeway. *I know next to nothing about him.* The large frame of the man was sitting

152

alongside her. She could feel his heat, smell his body. The odour of exertion, of honest, pedestrian labour; not unpleasant. *Except he's kindly and amusing and interesting – and he's a published writer! Yes, that's why you're doing this, Abi, my girl – and you don't even know that for sure. He could be shooting you a line.* But she believed him. His pack, almost as large as the man himself, was lying across the back seat. In a curious way it was reassuring; it lent legitimacy. The man was what he seemed: a simple traveller, like herself. Yes, she felt comfortable in his presence. Not the slightest bit threatened. She was curious, mind. She had hundreds of questions.

His accent, first. She was having trouble pinning it down.

"Aussie?" he cried. "Wash your mouth out, young lady!" Her eyes were on the road, but she could almost feel his mock indignation. "Quite near – but oh, so far! No, it's New Zealand. I'm from North Island – Bay of Plenty. Some would give you a smack for that mistake."

"And I would smack 'em back!" she rejoined. "At least I got the right half of the globe."

"You're forgiven," he said. He liked her spirit. In fact, he told himself, he liked everything about her. "My accent's perhaps not the easiest to pin down – and that's because I'm English. Spent over half my life in the UK. Didn't go to New Zealand till I retired."

"Retired from what?"

"Not important," he said.

"Okay – but why the secrecy?" She laughed. "Not a spy, were you?"

"No, nothing so exotic. What I did was satisfying. Valuable sometimes, I like to think. Just don't want to be defined by it. Never did. Sorry. There's what you *do,* and there's what you *are.* One's much more important than the other."

She had to be content with that. He really was a most unusual man. She had never had a conversation like this before. Quite extraordinary! But she was enjoying it, she found. Her guess was retired academic. Sociology, perhaps? Something like that. She had questions aplenty. "But whether I'll get answers," she thought, "is another matter. Perhaps he'd be more forthcoming about his writing?"

But he wasn't. Not immediately, anyway. This was mainly because he had questions of his own. Where and when was she born? (Tewksbury, 1989. *Hardly remember it; we moved around a lot.*) What university had she graduated from? (Leeds. *I did fine art. Loved the freedom, the chance to experiment – and that was just the social life!*) What of her parents, her family, her friends? (Father: died when she was fourteen; *I adored him.* Mother: still alive – *but we're estranged; she's impossibly neurotic.*) Was she in a relationship? (*Happily, no! Of the two most recent men in her life, the first was a complete wet, the other a complete arsehole!*) What made her happy, sad, angry? (In that order, she had turned up with *being in wild places, the death of my dad, even after ten years, and discourtesy; I hate discourtesy!*)

He seemed genuinely interested in all this. Interested in her. Unlike most men she'd met, he seemed happy to talk about her rather than about himself and his achievements. She liked that; it was refreshing. Yet it was also slightly frustrating because she was impatient to get to know him better – and because she was even more impatient to tap into his views about writing.

When they did get round to discussing writing – over coffee, after the meal – he was both relaxed and forthcoming. His views were thoughtful and measured, and they were delivered articulately, often with a dash of mischievous humour. He gave the impression that he was capable of speaking on different levels, that he could at any point go up or down a gear as required. Yet she never felt patronized, never felt that he was talking down to her. She was charmed.

"But why the short story?" she felt urged to ask. The lasagne had been seen off; she was pouring the coffee.

"Because it suits my temperament, I think. A novel is a burden, a monkey you carry on your back for two or three years. It chatters incessantly into your ear. Yes, it can be exciting – but it can also be wearisome, even to the point of dragging you down. Whereas with the short form, you can go from initial idea to decent first draft very quickly. In a matter of days sometimes."

"A bit like poetry?"

"A lot like poetry. The same immediacy, the same concision; the same imperative to make every word count. That's why poets often write good short stories, and why some short stories are almost like poems. Read Ted Hughes. Read his story called 'The Rain Horse'. Wonderful!"

"I will," she said. "Oh, so much to read! So much to learn! Not enough hours in the day."

"Yes, but try to be patient. You must write, you must read – but above all, you must live. And I think some of that living should be at the edges. Like your idol, Turner, if you like - lashed to the mast in a storm! That's a touch extreme for me, but it underlines the importance of first-hand experience."

"Ah, write about what you know? Isn't that what they say?"

"Yes, in a way. But writing comes from who you *are*. It comes from everything you've ever seen, ever thought, ever done, ever suffered, ever been uplifted by. It's recycled experience, if you like. We each have a unique way of looking at the world; and when we come to write about it, we each have a unique way of selecting and ordering the words. It's called your voice. It takes persistence and confidence to run with it. Some – the lucky, the really talented – find it quickly. It took me years."

"I'm just relieved that the words are coming," she sighed. "For the moment, I'll settle for that."

"Good. Patience is the name of the game, remember. And you start with an advantage. As an artist, you're used to observing. And you're used to looking at things from unusual, even quirky, angles – yes? Well, you're going to need that quirkiness as a writer. You're going to need the knack of making the familiar seem anything but familiar."

155

"That's another one for me to unpack later," she said, her eyes shining with excitement. "This is wonderful! Much more than I could have hoped for, really."

"Ah, so this is why you offer me shelter for the night," he laughed. "Forget altruism, forget charity, forget the goodness of your heart – the hope was that I would sing for my supper!"

"Oh, dear – I've been rumbled!" she laughed. "But can I get you to sing one last song?" He looked tired now, she thought; she didn't want to overtax him. "We must go to our beds, but can I ask one more question – if poetry and short fiction are as alike as you say, why have you settled on the short story all these years? Why aren't you a poet?"

"Good question," he replied. "I've written poetry on and off all my life. But writing poetry and claiming to be a poet are not one and the same. I'm drawn to the short story because, well, because I need a bit more landscape to work in, I suppose. And the story element's important for me; I seem to need a narrative. Characters, too. One or two – usually, no more. Characters who rub together, chafing, provoking thought, arousing emotion, causing a bit of aggro – of the sort that can be all over in three thousand words, or whatever. Not sure there's much more to say, really. Except I just love it – you know, the excitement, the uncertainty, that business of operating on the edge. And the immediacy, of course. I could go on, but it's been a long day – and you shouldn't encourage me. I could bore the pants off you!"

"No, you would never do that!" she protested. He smiled inwardly at her earnestness, her innocence. "It's wonderful to hear all this. There is just one more thing, though. She studied his face again and looked concerned. "No, no – I've kept you up long enough. We can talk about it in the morning."

"No, I'm all right – really I am. Fire away."

"Well, if you're sure? It's that word *uncertainty*. I don't know whether I can handle that. I do like to get things straight, organized. I like to know what's round the corner."

156

"But you've handled uncertainty through your art work, surely? When you start a painting, you never know the outcome I take it? The challenge of the empty canvas, the blank page: it's the same thing – yes?"

"Well, yes, I suppose you're right. I just never thought of writing in that way."

"That's the way it is, though. With fiction, certainly. Not like writing an essay, using notes. More like flying a kite."

"Flying a kite!"

"Well, I often think of the short story in that way. Like a child's kite. Not up for long, but it always captures a mood. Thought-provoking sometimes, as it hangs soulfully in the air. Amusing at other times, as it dances playfully about the sky. Not always easy to get up, mind. Or to keep up, for that matter. And as for ending its flight and bringing it safely to land – well, that can be even more testing."

"Fascinating!" she cried. "Lovely image. So if the story's a kite, what is poetry, then?"

"Oh, I don't know. Like a butterfly, perhaps? Suddenly appears, a brief flutter of colour, a striking impression and then it's away. Gone, almost as quickly as it came. Leaving us reflecting on its form, its beauty."

"And the novel?"

"Ah, more like an airship maybe? Yes, a large airship. With many compartments. Moving slowly. Full of people on a long journey, across a large landscape. Heavy on energy. Very difficult to get into the air. Quite vulnerable while it's up there – and attracting rather a lot of attention when it finally lands." He beamed across at her. "I should add that it has been known to crash – which is what happened to my four! And now, young lady, we really must go to bed." *Chance would be a fine thing*, he thought, and he smiled at the impropriety – then he thought ruefully of how long it had been. But thankfully, old men could still dream! They couldn't take that away from you.

Minutes later, James was listening at his bedroom door – listening for signs that Abi had finished in the bathroom. All now seemed quiet, so toilet bag in hand he stepped out — only to catch a brief view of her as she bounced across the hallway to her room. The image of her unfettered breasts dancing inside what appeared to be a white, man-sized shirt, punching it out, stayed with him long after he had put his light out.

He woke to the seductive smell of frying bacon and faint sounds of crockery clattering in the kitchen.

"Not New Zealand, I'm afraid," she said, as he appeared at the doorway, theatrically filling his lungs with the zest of the sizzling rashers. "Danish. Hope you're not offended. Help yourself to cereal, if you want that first. And there's plenty of toast and marmalade to follow. Now, tea or coffee?" She saw his face — wide-eyed, almost boyish with delight — and laughed. "Well, you need feeding up. The great sea voyage to Barragh — all half-an-hour of it! — demands a full stomach. Can't send you off adventuring, unfortified."

During the meal, between her comings and goings, they resumed the easy conversation of the night before. They talked a little about art and travel plans, but inevitably the subject moved on to writing. He wanted to know how much writing she had done.

"Oh, just sketches so far," she said. "I've stayed close to my art, I suppose. You know — observations, impressions, quick lines. Nothing meaty, nothing adventurous. Could be quite embarrassing when I get round to reading them. They'll probably end up in the bin."

"That would be a mistake," he advised. "First rule: never throw anything away. It can usually be cannibalized, or recycled, at some point later. And anyway, it's part of your writing history; it will indicate progress hopefully."

"I know what you're saying," she said. "Like my sketch books. I've kept them all." She paused and reached out to touch his wrist. "Thank you for that. Thank you for everything. I'm so grateful. So glad I met you."

"My pleasure," he said. She was reminding him more and more of his late wife. The same warmth, the same enthusiasm, the same wide-eyed innocence. Good in the kitchen, too. Claire wasn't as feisty, of course. And

158

not as spontaneous. "The gratitude's mutual," he added. "You've reminded me so much of, oh, I don't know, of a time when life was fresh and exciting and full of hope – a time when there was so much to see and do, with a whole lifetime in which to embrace it all. It has been a privilege for me, Abi, really it has."

"Really?" She looked genuinely surprised. "Oh, the time!" she cried, suddenly. "You mustn't miss that ferry."

She disappeared for two or three minutes, then reappeared, bursting in at the kitchen door all flushed with exertion from getting the car out of the lean-to garage.

"All ready?" she said. "It's almost time we weren't here."

He moved towards her and took both of her hands in his.

"This has been great," he said. "You've been so kind, so generous, taking me in like this."

"Not at all," she smiled, warmly. "It's been my pleasure. You're a lovely man, James. And last night was fascinating. I'll never forget it."

He let her hands fall away and moved in closer to give her a hug. She moved towards him and came into his embrace quite acceptingly. Her hair felt soft and silky against his cheek; it smelt of herb shampoo. Her body was warm and soft and pliant. He closed his eyes. It felt so good to be holding her. His left hand moved unconsciously down to her waist, and he pulled her in a little tighter. Yes, it felt good. So very good. *Oh, just a little while longer!*

Suddenly, abruptly, she pulled away. Rather, it was a pull at first; then it became a push. A very firm push away. He was alarmed at the strength of it – and even more disturbed by the look of surprise and bewilderment on her face.

"I'm sorry," she said, "but I wasn't comfortable with that. It was . . . " she was struggling "too . . . oh, I don't know . . . too intimate, I suppose."

"No, I'm the one who should be sorry," he said. "Forgive me. I forgot myself. It was strange. Like a moment from the past. A rather precious moment, if you want to know. But that's no excuse. It was clumsy of me. I

159

can understand how you might have found it . . . what's the word? Inappropriate. And I can only apologize if I've offended you."

"It's not . . . oh, I don't know really . . . I just didn't expect it, I suppose."

"From an elderly old bugger like me, you mean?"

"No . . . yes, something like that, I suppose. And I'm not so much offended as disappointed. It has kind of spoiled things, broken the spell. It can do that. Spoil things. Sex, I mean."

"I know what you mean," he said. "But you can't escape it, I'm afraid." He attempted a smile. "There is always sex – if only in the head." He picked up his gear and followed her sadly to the waiting car.

She had left the rear door open. Not for him to ride in the back, surely. He hoped not. He took a chance and stowed his pack on the back seat before levering himself into position alongside her.

"Again, I'm sorry," he said, turning to look at her. "I meant no ... you know? I never meant . . ."

"I know."

"Christ, I wish I could turn the clock back!"

"Me too, James."

Those lovely eyes of her had turned liquid. She looked so beautiful, so sad, so vulnerable. He wanted to take her in his arms again and hold her forever.

At the ferry terminal, a spit in the wind away from Bonnie Prince Charlie's Strand where they had met the previous day, they shook hands and she watched him trudge down the slipway towards the ramp. At the bottom of the slope he turned, and to his great relief he saw that she was waving.

"Good luck with the writing," he called back cheerily. "I shall look out for the name." He moved on and began ascending the ramp. Then suddenly he turned again and waved back. "Abyssinia!" he called.

LAS OREJAS

She first saw the ears in silhouette, lit theatrically from behind by intermittent flashes of lightning.

What a storm! More spectacular even than the one she had left behind when parting for the second time from Louis.

Their first parting had caused quite a storm, too. When it was over she had thought, naively, that she was rid of him. But the clever bastard had somehow managed to follow her to what she hoped would be a safe house in the Croaghgorms in County Donegal.

When he appeared – *for God"s sake, how had he managed to track her down like that?* – she had completely lost it. Shouting, screaming, storming about the house, crashing doors, hurling crockery – she had gone through the whole shooting match. She had even flashed a long kitchen knife at him, coming within a whisker of opening up his disbelieving face. In retrospect the thought of that had alarmed her; but her loss of control had been totally justified, she thought.

"The first time a man hits you, you may persuade yourself that perhaps you were partially at fault," the counsellor had advised, "but if there is a second time, the fault lies with him. It lies in his nature. He will probably do it again and again. Leaving him becomes the only option."

So she had fled him again, this time using a little legacy from her father to buy a renovated farmhouse in Las Alpujarras, a beautiful mountain range in Andalucia.

"Okay, Buggerlugs, see if you can find me now!" she laughed, as she drove to the head of a remote valley, where the *cortijo* lay tucked under the back wall of the mountain.

161

She called them *las orejas* – she was enjoying resurrecting her half-buried Spanish – because that was her first notion the night she arrived, the night of the storm. In outline, they looked just like the ears of animals grouped together above the rear wall of the terrace. Large ears. Pert ears. Prickly ears. Ears alert, listening for the next roll of thunder. In God's name, what sort – what *size*? – of animal grew ears as large, and as wide-set, as that! She had smiled at her racing imagination.

The next morning, of course, she saw them for what they were. *Las orejas* was certainly an obvious notion – but then, so was *los platos*. In fact, seen in the daylight, plates were perhaps a better image, for the cactus looked more like a piece of sculpture than a plant, she thought. More like a construction put together for a joke by a child – a child who enjoyed attaching one plate to another, setting them in improbable positions and at improbable angles; a child who was delighted by asymmetry, who wanted to see how far it was possible to build in one direction before her weird creation came toppling down.

She was delighted with her little hide-away. It was simple – primitive, some would say – but perfect for her needs. Electric power had not yet reached that end of the valley, so cooking, heating and lighting were dependent on container gas. However, the lack of modern services didn't worry her in the slightest. In fact, she was glad to escape all that. For one thing it added to the desired feeling of remoteness, the feeling of being shut off from the world. There, in the simplicity of her restored Berber farmhouse, whose thick stonewalls had escaped the modern tendency to whitewash, she was sure she could preserve her anonymity.

Everything about her situation was understated: the wild, high-valley setting; the humble, drab-grey *cortijo*; her unwashed, white Renault van which had replaced the smart VW Polo; her choice of subdued clothing, almost peasant-like in its simplicity. Yes, just like the tiny chameleon that had run across the ceiling when she first let herself in, she was sure she would soon merge into her background.

The cactus – *la chumbera*, they called it locally – was everywhere, she was to discover. Her property was ringed by single specimens; and downhill from her, on what had been a cultivated terrace in the days when every available strip of land thereabouts had been farmed, the plant had invaded so successfully that it now formed an impenetrable colony of interlocking branches. Further evidence of how easily the species could take over was to be found at the property nearest to hers, some three kilometres down the valley. A ruin now – uninhabited for nearly forty years – it was almost completely obscured by a weird jig-saw puzzle of barbed, green plates. The dark, broken lines of the *cortijo's* ancient chestnut timbers, just visible above the phalanx of prickly joints, were now the only signs of human habitation. She didn't know whether she should be disturbed or comforted by the thought that her nearest neighbour was a rampant cactus.

If she had entertained any doubts regarding how weatherproof her little farmhouse might be, they were dispelled on that first night. "The worst storm for twenty-five years!" she was to hear someone say at the market the following Thursday. But though the thunderous explosions seemed certain to lift her roof off, though the wind seemed to be rattling the life out of her shutters, and though the rain, when it came, caused floods to fly horizontally from her waterspouts, not a stone was disturbed, not a fitting was broken, and not a drop of water found its way into the house.

She needn't have worried: those Berber migrants knew a thing or two about house-building. Thick slabs of stone formed the walls of the traditional *cortijo*, and the chestnut-timbered flat roof was topped with sheets of slate sealed with *launa*, a local mica clay, that became water-tight when tamped down. In the old days, she learned, the

163

launa could only be laid down during a waning moon. She liked the idea of that; it lent a touch of magic to the place.

For her, more magic – or perhaps *charm* was a better word – was added by the short, squat chimney pots protruding through the roof. Commonly, a *cortijo* would have only one chimney – at most, two – but for some eccentric reason she was blessed with three, each one wearing a comical, flat-brimmed stone hat. They reminded her of the hats Boy Scouts used to wear. "Pleased to meet you, lads," she smiled, when she saw them on that first morning. "Thanks for helping to keep my roof on. Stick around, eh? There could be a bob or two in it for you." She was enchanted by her chimneys; they would be her loyal guards, her friendly look-outs. There and then, instead of *Cortijo de Buena Vista* – which anyway she thought was a bit naff; far too touristy – she renamed the house *Las Chimeneas*.

She loved her little farmhouse. Loved the way it seemed to be a natural part of the mountain wall – almost as if, rather than being built, it had taken growth there. Except for *las chimeneas*, of course: they stuck out somewhat unnaturally, she had to concede. A bit like cairns. But that was only when you got up close; from a distance they were little more than smudges of rock, merging in.

Most of all, she loved the *cortijo's* location. Lower down, where the valley flattened out, the land was still farmed. People could be seen working in the fields, bent low over their crops; and old-fashioned little tractors, looking like children's toys, could be heard chugging to-and-fro. But at her end, the valley sides were too steep for modern farming. A succession of narrow terraces stepped down to the river far below; they hadn't been worked since the more remote *cortijos* were abandoned, but here and there traces of the old irrigation system could be picked out. The scene helped create for her a sense of timelessness and mystery.

She felt totally relaxed in the seclusion of this setting. She loved the way she could sometimes go for days without seeing a single soul.

Apart from days when she was forced to steal anonymously into the nearest town for supplies, she could enjoy the feeling that she was lost to the world. Lost without trace, she hoped, immediately dismissing an image of Louis's face made hideous by anger.

As time wore on – as she learned to manage her housekeeping a little more astutely – she found herself driving into town less and less frequently. And when she did venture forth, she tried if she could to avoid the Thursday street market. It attracted too many people, too many tourists, too many opportunities for being noticed; it presented a far likelier risk of being recognized. Although she did everything she could to avoid drawing attention to herself – dressing like a local, speaking like a local (her degree-level Spanish had quickly acquired a regional, idiomatic dimension), even driving an unwashed van that made her *look* like a local – she knew that one freak encounter could blow her cover.

The ubiquitous cactus never ceased to fascinate her. It was a much more prominent feature higher up the valley; but even lower down, among the houses that fringed the narrow road leading into the small town, it had been introduced to form screens and barriers in much the same way that hedges were used back in England.

However, it was the wild, out-of-control formations to be found higher up in her part of the valley that engaged her most. Her first impression – that of *las orejas* – had stayed with her. It was hardly surprising: some of the joints in the strange, auricular articulations she studied so closely were even curved inwards like ears. And like her father's ears, they bristled. She suddenly had a picture of herself sitting on Daddy's knee, staring intently at the side of his face, and gently fingering the hair that had fought its way out of the darkness into the light.

So many ears! Thousands and thousands of them in her part of the valley alone. All listening. Her friends, all of them. Listening on her

165

behalf. Listening for the slightest sound of an approach. With *las chimeneas* keeping watch and *las orejas* listening out, Louis could never approach without warning. The thought helped to allay a fear that never quite left her.

One day she noticed a change in *la chumbera*: small, yellowy buds had erupted at the edges of the ears. The buds grew larger and larger, until in a week or two they were the size of small pears. Eventually they swelled so much, and their skins became so tight, that they ruptured slightly, offering a hint of their blood-red insides. A short time later, they began to drop off and fall to the ground. They looked succulent, good enough to eat. Were they edible, she wondered?

"*Los chumos*? Yes, yes, you can eat them," laughed the senora. It was the following morning. Sylvia had made one of her rare trips to town and had found the fruits displayed in a tray alongside the peppers inside one of the small stores used mainly by locals. "Of course you can eat them. Why I sell them, if not for eating?"

But raw, or cooked? Sylvia had turned away, unwilling to expose her ignorance any further. Perhaps better to play it safe? Yes, she decided, she would cook them.

And so it was that she drove back up her valley and collected a handful of *los chumos*. She scooped up the pears eagerly and dropped them into a pan. It wasn't till she got back into the house that she realized her mistake.

Unlike the ear-like pads from which they grew, *los chumos* had appeared to be smooth; but in fact they were covered in tiny, barbed hairs – and rather like small splinters, they were painful. Not unbearably: nothing like that. More of an insistent irritation – a bit like midge bites. Seeking relief, she tried rubbing her palms on the bone of her knees, and on the bone of her elbows – anywhere hard, in a desperate attempt to ease the discomfort.

166

"How stupid of me," she cried, scratching the back of her neck, as she was wont to do when perplexed or exasperated.

When no relief came, she had resorted to the pan-scrubber. She was desperate. In fact, it took several days of bathing and scrubbing and scouring before she was rewarded with pain-free hands.

Despite this experience, she was determined to go ahead and cook the pears. Handling them now with great caution – she had put on thick gardening gloves – she first dropped them into boiling water, hoping to destroy the barbs, or at any rate disarm them. After three or four minutes, she fished one out and tested it gingerly with a bare finger. It had worked! *El chumo* was tamed. It was now as smooth as a baby's bottom. She was delighted with herself – so much so that she felt emboldened to taste the pear just as it was.

The flesh tasted weakly sweet – not unlike that of watermelon – but it had to be sieved through the teeth to avoid the numerous seeds. Cooking it for longer seemed to reduce the sweetness, she discovered; it also helped to release the seeds which could then be strained off. All in all, it was a successful experiment; and in the days that followed, while the harvest lasted, she ate kilos and kilos of *los chumos*.

"All this," she cried, standing outside *Las Chimeneas* one day and looking across her beautiful valley to the elegant line of the ridge beyond, " – all this, and food for free into the bargain. What a magical place this is."

It started as an itchiness on the back of her neck. She thought nothing of it at first, though she began to tire of scratching it. Then she felt a small bump, a slight enlargement on what she laughingly called her dowager's hump. She was rather self-conscious about this knobbly bit of her spine, and was alarmed at the thought of it becoming any more pronounced. But still she thought little of it. Perhaps the scratching had caused the swelling? Or maybe, without noticing it, she had knocked herself on the headboard of the bed. She tried to dismiss the bump. After all, there was no one but her to see the disfigurement – and at least it was no longer itching.

But the swelling grew bigger and bigger, fanning out from her neck until the top could be seen well above the level of her head. Surprisingly, the growth wasn't heavy. At this stage it was like a large, thin, oval wafer; it reminded her, as she inspected it daily in the mirror, of one of those elaborate mantilla combs that Spanish ladies used to wear. Except it was solid, not lacy – and it was green!

She rather liked it. She was only too aware that she had tended to let herself go recently, but now she was transformed. Her splendid green mantilla added an exotic – perhaps, quixotic? – touch to her appearance. It was a bit inconvenient, of course – especially when she lay down to sleep – but one couldn't have everything in this life, she had to remind herself.

Oddly, her calm acceptance of this extravagant appendage seemed not to surprise her. She had been feeling rather strange lately. Not exactly ill. Just a bit peaky, that was all. No appetite, for one thing; she had gone off meat and fish altogether. She felt lethargic, too – constantly, though she had put this down to not eating properly. Her complexion was changing: that was another thing. Her skin was turning a yellowish-green, giving her a look of being perpetually sea-sick. "Probably all the *chumos* I've been eating," she had joked. It didn't seem to bother her at all. Nothing did. There was no tension. Not a muscle twitched. She felt totally relaxed.

Subsequent growths developed, first on her knees, then on her elbows; protruding almost at right angles, they made movement increasingly difficult. Not that she felt much inclination to move. So when more pads grew out from her feet and ankles, making walking almost impossible, she accepted her condition with a stoic calm.

Her hands were the last part of her limbs to be affected. Large green pads, looking like thick table tennis bats, now stuck out from them. She might have worried about her ability to feed herself –

168

except by now she wasn't entirely certain where her mouth was, and in any case she had absolutely no interest in food. She hadn't eaten a thing for weeks. How she was keeping going was a mystery. The only thing she craved was sunlight, and it wasn't long before she was spending all her time outside in the courtyard. The sunshine seemed to be sustaining her. It was weird. Was she photosynthesizing, she wondered? Was that why she had developed this strong, heliotropic tendency? It seemed a fantastical notion – yet how else could it be explained that, despite not eating, she was still alive and well, and growing fast?

In the weeks that followed, her transformation continued. She now had prickly pads projecting from all parts of her body, and was even sprouting pads on her pads! She had long since lost the use of her limbs; as far as she could tell, her lower regions appeared to have atrophied. It was hard to see what was happening down there because, having grown so tall, her seeing parts were almost three metres away. But as far as she could see through the tangle of pads, her legs seemed to have fused together and acquired a vague, dusty-grey, woody appearance.

Far from being alarmed, she was enjoying her vegetative state. Totally stress-free, she rejoiced in her novel condition and the unhurried pace of life it imposed on her. She was particularly delighted that she had grown a pair of ears of her own: big, giant teddy bear's ears that curved inwards, good for listening.

By now she had branched out in all directions and was taking up a sizeable part of the courtyard. In the space left, she was able to practise a novel form of movement – for she had discovered a new, exciting skill. If she concentrated hard on a particular part of her new-fangled anatomy, she could build up tension to such a point that a new pad would sprout. In this way, she could develop so far in one direction that eventually balance was lost, and she would rock over into a new position.

169